T0018169

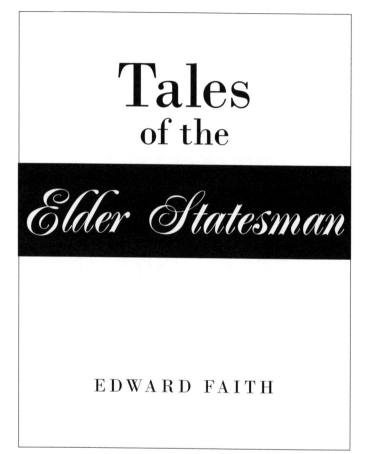

Tales
of the
Elder Statesman

EDWARD FAITH

TALES OF THE ELDER STATESMAN

iUniverse books may be ordered through booksellers or by contacting:

iUniverse
1663 Liberty Drive
Bloomington, IN 47403
www.iuniverse.com
844-349-9409

ISBN: 978-1-6632-0708-1 (sc)
ISBN: 978-1-6632-0709-8 (e)

Library of Congress Control Number: 2021905032

Print information available on the last page.

iUniverse rev. date: 03/15/2021

Contents

Speechless

My wife and I once had a postal contract. One part of that contract required us to pick up the mail and bring it to the post office in Rough Edge each morning. The postmaster in Rough Edge was notorious for arriving at work in a furious rush each morning at eight o'clock. Each morning we would stop by the only store in Rough Edge and get a cup of coffee while we waited for the postmaster to go speeding by.

It so happened that I was in the store on the first day of school, leaning against a stack of feed sacks, drinking my coffee. At that particular hour on that particular day, seven or eight mothers and their children were in the store, rushing around getting paper, pencils, and snacks. Quite a hubbub was going on among the mothers and children when the door opened and in walked the Elder Statesman. Being the gentleman that he was, starting with the first mother he encountered, he went all the way around the store, speaking to each of them, shaking their hands, and patting the children on their heads. He was in his element, for the Elder Statesman was a verbose person, never at a loss for words. He worked his way around the store, finally reaching the end of the counter near where I stood. He was beaming as he looked around to be sure he had not missed anyone.

Seeing that his speaking tour was complete, I called to him, "Hey, come over here. I need to talk to you for a minute."

We walked over to where the coffee pot was located and away from everyone else in the store.

Looking around to be sure no one else could hear, I said to him in a low but serious tone, "Have you noticed that all the women in the store are in a nervous twitter this morning?"

Glancing over his shoulder at all the mothers frantically trying to get their business transacted so they could get to school on time, he replied, "Yeah, I see what you mean. What you reckon is going on?"

With a most serious expression on my face and deep gravity in the tone of my voice, I put my hand on his shoulder and, drawing him up close, said to him, "Well, I cannot be absolutely certain, but if I were you, I would zip my pants."

A shocked look immediately replaced the radiant glow on his face. Looking down to confirm the reality of the situation, he looked as if he had bitten into a very sour lemon. He didn't say another word that morning but tore away from me and, in a near run, left the store, jumped into his pickup, and sped away for home. It was the only time I ever saw the Elder Statesman speechless.

A Bald Head and Witty Banter

Watson was a jovial, fun-loving guy who worked at one of the big hardware stores in Mobile. He knew people from all over southern Alabama, having made the acquaintance of thousands through his work. The Elder Statesman was one of those acquaintances and had become a very close friend. Watson often came up to Washington County to go hunting with him. The Elder Statesman's place was wedged between Rough Edge and Harvey's Creek and had some of the best deer and turkey hunting in the country.

Early one morning in the spring gobbling season, Watson and the old man set out for an area where they had heard turkeys fly up the evening before. Watson did not get very much exercise where he worked. The long trek through the woods just about winded him. Watson's heavy breathing was getting on the Elder Statesman's nerves.

Turning around, he said in a scolding tone, "Watson, you quit that breathing."

"If I do, I'll die!" exclaimed the alarmed hunter.

Later, with one fine gobbler in the bag, the two hunters returned to camp for coffee and breakfast. The brisk spring morning air and the long trek had given the hunters a ravenous appetite. The Elder Statesman washed up and began cooking bacon, eggs, and biscuits while the aroma of fresh coffee filled the camp.

As breakfast was being prepared, Watson changed from his hunting togs to more comfortable casual clothes. Coming into the kitchen, he took a seat at the table to sip at his coffee. Except for his mustache-covered upper lip, his freshly washed face and bald head were shining in the bright kitchen light.

"One bright light in here was enough, Watson. Did you have to polish that bald head of yours so that it would shine?" the Elder Statesman said.

The glib hardware man countered while rubbing his bald head and stroking his mustache, "I suppose you don't like my mustache either, but everyone knows when you clear up eighty acres, you run a cross fence."

Such was the bantering Watson and the Elder Statesman carried on.

A Bunch of Howling Mutts

The sobriquet "Foots" adequately described the large dimension of the terminus of Jimmy's lower appendages. The Elder Statesman did not remember the numerical size of the man's shoes, but when Jimmy played the guitar, he did not pat his foot to keep time; he only patted his toes. He was under medical supervision for an excitable emotional condition that required medication for him to function normally. Jimmy's thought patterns did not run in the same paths as most other folks'. They did not even assume a parallel course. They broke out in random places concerning whatever Jimmy was working on at the time.

Jimmy, having grown up in rural Culp County, decided like many others with similar backgrounds to raise some poultry for his own consumption. He purchased twenty biddies, brought them home, and installed them in a fifty-five-gallon, open-top drum, intending to build a pen and a brooder for them on the upcoming weekend. Upon hearing about the poultry project at work, the Elder Statesman informed Jimmy that biddies had to be kept warm.

"Hang a light in the drum about eighteen inches above the biddies, and that will keep them warm enough," said the old man.

Two days later, Jimmy reported, "When I came home from work, all my biddies were flat on their backs with their feet sticking up in the air, stone dead. I did not unplug the light, and in the hot part of the day, they overheated and died. I guess I cooked them too soon."

After Jimmy's poultry project concluded, he moved to Carter's Corner.

A bleary-eyed, yawning Jimmy came into the Elder Statesman's office one Monday morning.

"What's wrong with you?" inquired the Elder Statesman.

"My neighbor has two or three dogs, and they barked all night, keeping me awake!" exclaimed Jimmy.

The subsequent nights proved to be repeat performances by the dogs. Jimmy came across an advertisement in the Mobile paper for some double-pane windows guaranteed to reduce outside noise. Jimmy called the business offering the windows and arranged for them to be installed on his house.

A few days afterward, Jimmy came to work with a scowl creasing his face, complaining, "Those windows are no good. Those dogs are still keeping me awake! I called that company and told them to come get those windows out of my house. They said the windows were a quality product that performed as advertised, they were never said to soundproof a house, and they would not take them back or refund my money! Worse than spending $1,700 for windows that don't work," cried Jimmy, "I still stay awake, listening to a bunch of howling mutts!"

A Cheap Lesson Learned

Without a doubt, Russ Jones—a big African American working at the same plant as the Elder Statesman—loved beer, which was evidenced by his profuse sweating even on cold days. The consumption of beer added many aluminum cans to those he collected and sold. Over time, Russ pocketed around $1,600 from his can sales, with which he intended to have a right jolly ole time.

One weekend, Russ ventured forth to the mobile home of three ladies of questionable virtue. In the course of the evening, his predisposition to drink beer soon placed him in an inebriated state. The three ladies, having promoted the overindulgence, took advantage of the situation to relieve Russ of his $1,600, after which they escorted him out of the mobile home. Russ made it back home, only to discover his loss once the effects of his drinking subsided. He was determined to get his money back.

Russ called his friend Joe and pleaded with him to, "Take me to Mount Morgan to get my money back. Those three women got me drunk and rolled me."

Joe cautioned, "You had better stay away from down there, Russ. That might be a cheap lesson they taught you!"

Russ was angry and insistent that Joe take him to confront the women. Joe finally agreed to drive Russ to Mount Morgan. When they reached the mobile home, Russ got out of the car, yelling at the three women who were sitting outside that he had come for his money and they had better give it to him. The ladies got up and went inside with Russ following them, still loudly demanding his money. Only seconds after going inside, Russ came running out with one of the women right behind him, slashing at him with a large butcher knife.

Russ didn't have time to open the door and get into the car. Instead he ran around it screaming, "Open the door, Joe! Open the door!"

Joe was laughing so hard, he was helpless, but after Russ had circumnavigated the car five times, Joe got a door open, and Russ dove into the safety of the vehicle, locking the door behind him.

With eyes bulging in panic, Russ cried, "Let's go, Joe! Come on! Let's go!"

It was sometime after they headed up Highway 45 before Russ settled down. Reaching into his pocket, he brought out a small pocketknife and opened its one broken blade, which was about an inch long. He said to Joe, "It's a good thing you got me away from there before I had to cut one of those women!"

Joe's eyes widened incredulously.

A Day in the Life of a Foreman

The Elder Statesman leaned back in his chair and, kicking his feet up onto the desk, mused about the strange events he had witnessed at work.

Caspar was a problem child. He had been shuffled around all over the plant. No matter what area he worked in or which foreman he worked for, he generated difficulties. Finally, he had been shifted to traffic and into the crew of the Elder Statesman. Caspar's reputation preceded him. True to form, he began creating problems. However, one problem was purely accidental.

The foremen picked up the crew's checks from payroll every Friday afternoon around one o'clock. Most of the time, they passed the checks out a few minutes before the shift ended, and the men went home. Not wanting to leave checks unattended in the office, the Elder Statesman had given his men their checks shortly after he picked them up. He went to warehouse 505 where Caspar was putting sticky back labels on fifty-five-gallon steel drums. The old man handed Caspar his check as he rode by on his bike and then rode on to pass out the rest of them.

When Caspar finished labeling the drums, he came to the office and said, "I need you to get me another check."

Alarmed, the Elder Statesman asked, "Why? I gave you one less than an hour ago!"

Caspar explained, "I had a label in my hand with the back peeled off when you came by and gave me my check. I was looking at the check when a gust of wind blew in the warehouse door, causing the label to flop around and into my check. It stuck immediately, covering most of the back of the check," said Caspar. "I tried to peel it off, but my check kept getting lighter and lighter, so I brought it to you."

The Elder Statesman took the check and label combination, reached into his desk drawer, retrieved a pair of scissors, and trimmed the tenaciously stuck label from around the check.

"Take the check like this and see if you can get it cashed," said the old man. "It is too late to get another one today. If you can't get it cashed, I'll get you another one tomorrow."

A smiling Caspar came in the next morning and said, "They cashed it!"

The Elder Statesman often wondered what the payroll personnel had thought when that check came back through.

Resins in a multitude of formulations were manufactured in the plant. The Elder Statesman warehoused and shipped those products. A few of the formulations were packaged in fifty-five-gallon lock ring drums. These drums had removable tops that were held in place by a steel locking ring. Norvel was assigned the loading of a trailer with resin in lock ring drums.

When he was about half-done, Norvel carried two drums up the loading ramp with drum clamps. Drum clamps had two hooks that lifted the drums by the locking rings. Someone in production had failed to tighten the locking rings on those two drums. When Norvel went over the hump at the top of the loading ramp, the tops popped off the drums and the drums turned over, spilling 110 gallons of very sticky resin in the trailer. It took a pallet of oil dry to soak up the stuff in the trailer. However, the resin had seeped into every crack and crevice, sealing the floor of that trailer airtight. The Elder Statesman whispered a prayer of thanks that the spilled resin was not classed as flammable!

A Driving Lesson at Rattlesnake Forks

Aliens, strangers, foreigners find it difficult to be assimilated into the culture of Rough Edge. It's not that the citizenry of that humble burg isn't friendly, but they tend to be just a wee bit clannish. Years passed before A.D. Jones and his family became accepted like they were old-line residents. By that time, their children—four boys—were grown and gone. The boys had married and started families of their own. Over time, they made trips home to see their parents.

The Elder Statesman got off work at 3:20 p.m., and thirty minutes later, arrived in Rough Edge. On the way to his house, the old man was going to turn off Highway 24 onto County Road 38 at an intersection known far and wide as Rattlesnake Forks. It got that name because local people hung most of the rattlesnakes killed in and around Rough Edge on the stop sign at that intersection. He saw a strange car sitting at that stop sign. As he approached to make his turn, he looked at the driver of the strange car. It was a woman who had a fierce grip on the steering wheel, with her arms rigidly locked at the elbows. Her eyes were unblinkingly fixed in a straight-ahead stare. Her mouth was slightly open, and the skin of her face was ghostly white.

The Elder Statesman knew something was bad out of kilter with that woman. After seeing her, he ran about a hundred feet past her car before he could stop. Pondering what could be wrong, the old man believed that the woman must be on some kind of drug. He looked back at the intersection, but there was no vehicle was in sight.

Something crazy is going on here, he thought. *No car could get out of sight that quick.* That awe-stricken man backed up to the stop sign, got out of his car, and looked up and down the highway, but no other car was to be seen or heard.

Then he noticed that the weeds and brush on the shoulder of Highway 24 were mashed down somewhat just past the intersection. Momentarily, he heard a scuffling sound down in that deep brush-covered ditch.

"Hey, are you all right down there?" yelled the Elder Statesman.

"Yeah, we are OK. We will be up there soon as I get my wife out of the car."

The old man knew instantly that it was Carlton Jones because he had a unique Southern accent that was drawn out unusually long.

"Is that you, Carlton?" the old man asked.

When the somewhat-shaken couple reached the road, Carlton answered in the affirmative.

"What in the world happened?" asked the Elder Statesman.

"We were down here to see Mom and Dad. This being out in the country with little traffic on the roads, I decided it would be a good time and place to teach my wife to drive. She was terrified that she would do something wrong and have a wreck. When we got to the intersection, I told her to stop, which she did. Looking both ways and seeing no traffic after you turned, I told her to go on and turn right. Before I could tell her to straighten up in the highway, she held the car in the turn and ran off into the ditch. The car went out of sight in the bushes," Carlton said.

"She looked panic-stricken to me." The Elder Statesman laughed. "You really do need to teach her to drive. Get in and I will take you home."

Carlton replied, "Thanks, but take me out to the county commissioner's house. He has equipment he can use to pull my car out of the ditch."

A Good Fight

H ank, "the Animal," Fleming was a boxer of some renown a few decades ago who protested that he could not enjoy a fight until he felt pain. A sports commentator broadcasting one of Hank's fights said, "Hank must really be enjoying this fight. He is getting knots all over his head." Such a mentality was not unique to Hank.

Down in the nether regions of Manchester, where the fringe elements of society congregated, lived a malefactor by the name of Gerald Warren. Gerald was not a big man. He was about five feet six and 160 pounds. He kept his head shaved and attired himself in jeans and polo shirts. Numerous scars gave emblematic testimony of his one joy in life, namely a good fight. Gerald frequented all the joints and dives in Manchester.

The Morocco Palace was one such establishment. The owner and manager at the time had a broken leg, which doctors had put in a cast. Over a period of six weeks, Gerald had instigated a fight in the Palace at least two nights a week, resulting in most of the clientele seeking refreshments in other watering holes. Some change was going to have to be made.

Saturday night when Gerald walked into the sparsely populated Morocco Palace, the manager called him over to the bar and said to him, "Why don't you go somewhere else? You have run off most of my patrons, and I would leave myself if my leg wasn't broken."

Gerald looked around at the few customers and, not seeing any prospect of a fight, replied, "You know, I think I will go elsewhere. There's no action going on here." He left looking for a better haunt to terrorize.

North of Manchester was a naval air station that sported a large canteen. It proved to be just the place Gerald was seeking. After an hour of sitting at the bar, consuming a beer now and then, he was getting bored when an altercation broke out between two sailors. Within a few minutes, it became a melee involving most of the men in the place.

An inspired Gerald jumped up on the bar and shouted above the din, "Wait a minute! Wait a minute!" In the momentary silence, he then cried, "Let's do this thing up right. Let's go outside and choose up."

Bruised, battered, and bloody men in the parking lot were taking wild swings at each other when the police arrived with lights flashing. The Elder Statesman watched as the police loaded the participants into four paddy wagons and hauled them off to jail. Gerald, smiling that toothless grin of his as he stepped up into the paddy wagon, had found his kind of place.

A Nervous Eye
on Lillian

The Elder Statesman had several profitable business ventures. However, the income from them did not flow in a steady stream; it came in sizable chunks at various times. Hence, there arose days when he needed cash but didn't have any on hand. On one such occasion, he went to Ole E.D., a family friend, and borrowed two hundred dollars.

"I have a retirement check coming next week," he said. "I'll pay you back when I get it."

Ole E.D. and his wife, Lillian, ran a mail route. They stopped most mornings at the only store in Rough Edge to get a cup of coffee and sometimes a snack. It just so happened that Lillian was running the mail route a week later and stopped at the store for coffee. The store sold hoop cheese encased in red wax by the slice. Lillian bought a slice of cheese and some crackers for a snack that day. Mrs. Irma cut her a half-pound slice, wrapped it in butcher paper, and handed it to her.

At that moment, the door opened and in walked the Elder Statesman. Lillian said to him, "All right. I saw your retirement check come through the mail yesterday. Now pay me the two hundred dollars you owe us."

"I haven't got it. I've already spent it," he declared.

A half pound of cheese was more than Lillian wanted at one time, so she planned to cut it in half and save part of it for later. To do so, she asked Mrs. Irma, "Where's your knife?"

The Elder Statesman, not knowing about the cheese, thought Lillian was getting the knife after him. He was so shaken up that he almost tore the pocket out of his pants getting out his billfold. With a shaking hand, he handed her two crisp one-hundred-dollar bills.

"Thank you," Lillian said.

From that time on, the Elder Statesman kept a nervous eye on Lillian whenever he was in her presence.

A Rainy Gaff

It doesn't rain in the army. It rains on the army. Those who have served a hitch with Uncle Sam know that to be a fact. McDonald was as country as a man can be coming out of the hills of Culp County. He enlisted in the same company of the Alabama Army National Guard in which the Elder Statesman served as company clerk. McDonald was assigned to the cooks' section. He liked his assignment to the cooks because they started three hours before the other troops and were finished when the kitchen was cleaned up after dinner—a schedule he was accustomed to living in the country.

Each year, the company was sent to a regular army post for two weeks of active duty training. They set up and operated as if they had been called up for active duty. The unit was a petroleum depot company that operated pipelines and manifolds, a setup of pipes and valves through which petroleum could be diverted into any of several pipelines. Regular army advisers helped direct the training and graded the unit on its performance.

One rainy midmorning, one of the advisers, a colonel, came over to the company headquarters to confer with the CO. When an officer enters a building, the first person to see him is supposed to call everyone to attention. The colonel had on a raincoat and a plastic cover over his cap, which left no insignia visible. McDonald was standing by the door as the officer approached. He opened the door and held it open but, seeing no insignia, did not call attention.

Instead, he said to the colonel, "Come on in, cuz, and have a cup of coffee."

All was well, however, as the CO called us to attention and the colonel himself could not help but laugh at McDonald's gaff, saying to him, "I believe I will. Bring me a cup."

Unusual things sometimes happen when it rains on the army.

A Rare Tale

Consternation was bleeding over into pandemonium among the constituents of the small crowd gathered at Rattlesnake Forks on the west side of Rough Edge. The Elder Statesman, in a rare celebratory mood, had imbibed an excess amount of whiskey and under its influence had wandered off into the woods, carrying the half-empty bottle with him. After the passage of several hours, his family became concerned when he failed to return home. They spread an alarm to friends and other family members to meet up at Rattlesnake Forks and begin searching for the old man.

Just east of Rattlesnake Forks, on the north side of Highway 24, is a small mill pond. When Highway 24 was paved, a cement culvert four feet wide and five feet high was poured under the road to take care of water draining from the pond. The Elder Statesman had stooped over and wiggled his way into the culvert to consume the rest of the bottle's contents undisturbed.

One of the people in the crowd suggested that they begin calling for the Elder Statesman in hopes that he would answer them. Forthwith, there broke out a racket that would have done a group of cheerleaders justice. The old man in the culvert, even in his jovial state, realized they were searching for him, so he decided to have a little fun at their expense.

He crept down to the north end of the culvert, turned around, and yelled back through that cement tunnel, "Help, help, help! Help me!"

Yelling back through the culvert projected his voice to sound as if it were a quarter of a mile down in the woods south of the highway. The gathered troops set off in search of the old man, tromping through brush and brambles for over an hour and winding up a ragged, scratched, and exhausted group.

Meanwhile, the Elder Statesman had wiggled down to the south end of the culvert. He turned around and yelled the same words back through it. The electric effect of the words energized the crowd, setting them off in a stampede north of the road this time. Of course, their search was futile, yet the old man was enjoying himself immensely.

After the third rampage into the woods, one person in the crowd figured out what was happening. He led a few of the less excited people present down to the culvert, from which they retrieved the laughing Elder Statesman. He was the only completely refreshed person in the gathering at Rattlesnake Forks. The severely tested friendships survived intact as the members of the crowd realized they had been handed a rare tale with which they could regale their grandchildren.

The Elder Statesman nonchalantly dropped the empty bottle into the trash can.

An Eye for Talent

T alent, the stuff of which genius is made, is distributed all through the human population, finding expression in many disciplines. Howard Hill could shoot a flying hawk clutching a dove with a bow and arrow without hitting the dove. He could shoot an arrow into a bull's-eye and then, shooting again, split the first arrow with the second. Beethoven could tune a piano more accurately by ear than most piano tuners could with tuning forks. In the pistol shooting competition at the Olympic Games, George S. Patton once fired six bullets through the same hole. Albert Einstein developed the theory of relativity by envisioning himself as a light beam traveling through space.

Alfred, a cross-eyed musician gifted on the fiddle and guitar, whose abode perched on a roadside bluff halfway up Simon Hill in the village of Rough Edge, taught quite a few locals to play both instruments. Coleen, a local piano teacher, wanted to learn to play the guitar, so she engaged Alfred to teach her. Coleen's piano playing was technically correct but mechanical. There was no variation, no passion, no creativity, but it was precise. The stage was set for a struggle because Alfred played strictly by ear and Coleen, though she had an ear for music, played strictly by note.

After the passage of some months, Coleen lamented to the Elder Statesman how frustrating her guitar lessons were. "When we are practicing, Alfred never plays a song the same way twice. That makes it so difficult for me to follow him."

The Elder Statesman asked, "Do you know why he is one of the best guitar players in these parts?"

"No, I don't," said Coleen.

The old man explained, "Being cross-eyed, he is the only person I know who can see both hands at the same time when he is playing the guitar."

Coleen's jaw dropped upon hearing such an incredulous statement, cementing her with rigid facial fixity.

Backseat Driver

Do not look on wine when it is red,
When it sparkles in the cup,
When it swirls around smoothly,
At the last it bites like a serpent,
And stings like a viper.
Your eyes will see strange things,
And your heart will utter perverse things.
                    — Proverbs 23:31–33,
                    New King James Version

T erry had just gone to bed when the telephone
      ringing assaulted his ears.

"I may as well get up and answer it or I will not get any sleep," Terry muttered to himself.

Upon answering the phone, he immediately recognized the voice of the Elder Statesman, who lived out on the western side of Rough Edge. Concern echoed in his voice as he said, "Terry, your father came out here to see me several hours ago. We talked for a while, and about seven o'clock, he got up to go home. I went back into the house and watched TV until ten o'clock. Getting ready for bed, I went to lock the front door and noticed that your dad's car was still in my driveway. You need to come out here and get him. He was deep in the bottle and in no condition to drive."

Terry got up, wearily dressed, went out to his car, got in, and drove out to the Elder Statesman's house. He pulled up behind his dad's car, got out, and walked over to the vehicle. When he opened the door, his dad would have fallen out if Terry had not caught him.

"Son, I'm so glad to see you! I've been lost for days! When I finally found my car, I got in only to realize that someone had stolen my steering wheel, brake pedal, and gas pedal. I've been trying to go home for hours."

"No wonder you think someone stole your car's controls!" screamed Terry. "You are in the back seat."

Rough Edge is blessed with its characters.

Baling Wire and Flat Tires

Back in the days before instant gadgetry gratification, the Elder Statesman played a fiddle at all sorts of social gatherings. After playing for a dance at the Rough Edge school, he arrived home after midnight. His father confronted him, saying, "Son, you have to make up your mind today. Are you going to work for a living or play the fiddle to earn your keep? You can't stay up half the night and work too."

Looking wistfully at the fiddle he loved, the Elder Statesman put it in its case, put the case on a shelf in his closet, and never played it again. He became a man totally dedicated to the sweat of the brow. Over his life span, he became a wealthy cattle and timber man while maintaining his determination and independent ways.

Mr. Miller had a farm supply store and tractor dealership in Stapleton, Mississippi, where the Elder Statesman bought a butane-burning tractor and a hay baler that used wire to tie the bales. Moe L., his grandson, was employed to bushhog his pasture. The bushhog was a pull-behind type that had a tire mounted on each side. A problem occurred because of the baling wire.

Some of the wires were put on the truck and carried out of the field. Some were twisted around the tops of nearby fence posts. Some were carelessly tossed away and left on the ground in the field. When Moe L. ran over the wires left on the ground with the bush hog, the mower blades made shrapnel out of the wire and slung it outward with such force that it penetrated the bush hog's tires, causing them to go flat. Three days in succession, Moe L. had to stop bushhogging and fix flats. Because Moe L. was losing too much time fixing flats, the Elder Statesman took action to end that problem.

When Moe L. came in around dinnertime with yet another flat, the old man handed him the key to his farm truck and bid him, "Go fill the truck with gas and check the oil and water. By the time you get that done, I'll be out there."

The old man did not drive, and he never told Moe L. or anyone else where he was going. When they came to an intersection, he would point in the direction he wanted to go without saying a word. At the end of the driveway, he directed Moe L. to Rattlesnake Forks, then to Rough Edge, then to Leroy, then to Jackson, and finally to Dennis McGavin's Tire and Recapping.

Mr. McGavin came over to the truck and, in a friendly greeting, said, "Hello. How are you today? 'Tis great that you are looking so well."

The Elder Statesman didn't acknowledge anything Mr. McGavin said but gazed fixedly ahead. When the business owner finished speaking, the old man turned to him, rigidly stared straight into his eyes, and stated, "I want two tires that *will not* go flat!"

"We have some mighty good tires, but they don't make any that will not go flat," responded the tire dealer.

"Put the best two you have on those wheels in the body of the truck," said the old man.

Mr. McGavin mounted on the wheels two of the best automobile tires he had in the place. The Elder Statesman paid for the tires and had started to leave when Mr. McGavin spoke up: "I'll give you three dollars apiece for those old tires."

"Don't want to sell 'em! Don't want to sell 'em! the Elder Statesman said emphatically with an annoyed look on his face. Forthwith, he directed Moe L. back home.

Lightning had struck and killed a large pecan tree near the old man's tractor shed. He had the limbs gathered into a huge pile. Upon arriving at home, the Elder Statesman directed Moe L. to carry the old tires out to the pile and wait for him. The Elder Statesman procured a box of matches from the kitchen and, while going by his woodshed, collected a handful of splinters.

"Moe L., take these matches and splinters and start a fire in that pile of limbs," ordered the old man. Sitting down on a five-gallon bucket, he watched the blaze grow until it was about thirty feet high. "Take those old tires and throw them right up there," commanded the Elder Statesman, pointing at the high point of the blaze. "If they aren't any good to me, they aren't any good to anyone!" he growled.

Bumpy Roads and Plenty of Bones

Back in the Elder Statesman's younger days, the roads in and around the village of Rough Edge were atrocious tracks through a forested wilderness. During the rainy winter months, log trucks passing through the town cut ruts so deep that the rear-end housing between the back wheels of the trucks dragged the ground. Whatever side of the street you were on, there you remained because the ruts were so deep and muddy, crossing was nearly impossible.

The frontier aspect of Rough Edge was exemplified by the huge oak tree that stood in the middle of the street. Traffic going west passed by the tree on the north side, and those going east passed by the tree on the south side. The condition of the roads was such that, weather permitting, they were worked on frequently.

Simon Hill lay on the western fringe of the territory encompassed by Rough Edge. The road leaving town ascended Simon Hill. Half the length of the hill was composed of a blue marl clay that rain made so slick you could barely stand on it. In those days, men had to work on the roads a prescribed number of days each year. The county supplied the equipment and supervision. The Elder Statesman was serving his time working on the road over Simon Hill. Truckloads of base material had been dumped in a zigzag pattern in the road where the blue marl cropped out. They were going to spread the base material over the blue marl so that vehicles would have traction when climbing the hill in wet weather. The work crew was eating dinner when they heard the roar of Moody's pickup.

West of Rough Edge there was an acre or two just off the road to Churchwell known as the boneyard. In those times, when an individual had an animal die, the carcass was dragged out to the boneyard and left to the buzzards and decomposition. Over a few months' time, quite a collection of bones accumulated.

There was a fertilizer plant in Jefferson that ground up bones to add to their product. Twice a year, Moody went to the boneyard, loaded the bones into his pickup, and carried them to the fertilizer plant to sell. He had a load of bones and was headed to Jefferson when the road crew heard him coming. Moody always drove just as fast as the road permitted. Topping Simon Hill wide open, he saw the piles of base material when it was too late to stop. The pickup careened from pile to pile all the way down the hill, unloading bones at every mound.

When he finally got the truck stopped, Moody jumped out and, upon seeing his bones scattered all over the road, yelled, "Who am I going to sue for this?"

An inspired Elder Statesman yelled back, "I don't know, but you nearly had St. Peter for a lawyer!"

Cheese Nachos
and a Wasp

Some days running a mail route can be quite an adventure. The Elder Statesman and his wife, Lillian, carried the mail for the town of Rough Edge and its surrounding areas. Handling the mail is a six-day-a-week job; thus, they had hired a helper so that each of them could have a day off during the week. Glenda, the helper, was a rather large woman, and she was the old man's niece.

Glenda liked to stop at the only store in Rough Edge to get a drink and a snack, often a pack of cookies. Wanting a little variety in her life, one day she decided to get a drink and chips with nacho cheese dip. Glenda was not the most adroit person in Rough Edge. To handle the mail, the cheese dip, and the chips in the best of circumstances would have required three hands. In less than ten minutes, the Elder Statesman looked at Glenda, and his eyes nearly popped out of their sockets.

In that short time, she had managed to spread cheese dip all around her mouth and chin. The front of her blouse had a nice, even orange coating, along with all her fingers.

Needless to say, the mail she was putting out also got an ample share of the cheese dip. The old man turned around and carried Glenda back to the store so she could clean up.

When she came back to the car, he said to her rather harshly, "From now on, all you can have to eat while working on the mail is hard candy."

The Rough Edge mail route included a long stretch through some very flat, sandy land along Harvey's Creek. Over the years as the county crews worked that stretch, a mound of dirt over two feet high had built up on both sides of the road. One day as they neared a curve in that road, an eighteen-wheel log truck popped around the bend, fully loaded and wound up. They were so close, there was no stopping either vehicle. The Elder Statesman got partway up the mound of dirt and so did the truck driver. When they passed, they were so close that the old man could have reached out and rubbed the tires of the truck. Glenda had the mail for the next box in her hands when they met the truck.

With a sigh of relief, the Elder Statesman looked at Glenda and told her, "Boy, that was a close call."

Glenda was so frightened that she was twisting the mail in her hands back and forth.

"What are you doing to those folks' mail?" he demanded.

"If we had wrecked, I wanted to have the mail ready," she said in a trembling voice.

The Mobile Cutoff was part of the route served out of the Rough Edge Post Office. About halfway through the Cutoff lived a family that had built a new house across the road from their former residence—a very old, dilapidated structure now being used as a barn. The Elder Statesman pulled up to the mailbox so Glenda could serve it. He turned and was looking across the road at the old house, lamenting its deteriorated condition, when suddenly Glenda crashed into his side. For a moment he thought she had cracked some of his ribs.

"What are you doing?" he yelled.

With an air of innocence, she grinned and said, "There was a wasp in that box!"

"He wasn't going to bother you," the old man retorted.

"I know." Glenda chuckled. "But I can't stand that fluttering!"

Doing Ninety Miles an Hour Down a One-Wheel Wagon Road

The Old South was a café, service station, and tire repair place all rolled into one. It was in an ideal location just south of the intersection of Highway 80 and Highway 45 in Winston. Local people, shift workers, highway patrolmen, and politicians were regular patrons of the place.

Back in 1953, Penrod—a state representative—was in the Old South, seated at the loafers table, expounding upon some grandiose plans for improving the state of Alabama when the Elder Statesman and Daniel walked in and sat down beside him.

His excited voice could be heard all over the place, saying, "Yes, sir. We are going to build that four-lane highway from Mobile to Montgomery. Not only are we going to build it, but we are going to make it downhill in both directions."

Penrod had that glib, jocular manner of exaggeration that politicians find so useful. Voters knew he was exaggerating, but they loved to hear him speak and voted for him anyway. The Elder Statesman was an expounder of stories with legendarily elongated basic facts. The conversation at the loafers table soon became a contest between the Elder Statesman and Penrod for the telling of the greatest rubberized story. For more than two hours, first one and then the other reached back into his memory to retrieve long-forgotten lore. The other patrons had about reached the limit of their tolerance for such absurdities and had begun leaving for home. The Elder Statesman and Daniel concluded that, in the absence of an audience, they might as well go home too.

After getting to-go cups of coffee, the pair sauntered out the door, got into Daniel's pickup, and headed for Rough Edge. With the two sipping hot coffee, not much was said until they turned off Highway 57 onto the Mobile Cutoff. Daniel, with an aggrieved look at having had his intelligence insulted, remarked, "I knew Penrod was lying when he started talking about doing ninety miles an hour down a one-wheel wagon road."

The Elder Statesman smiled and nodded in agreement.

Don't Get Caught with Your Hand in a Potato Chip Bag

The event took place too long ago to even talk about. Nevertheless, because it led to the entry of an expression into the hunting lore around Rough Edge that the Elder Statesman and other old timers still use, I shall relate the details of how it came to be.

The Elder Statesman at this time lived at the end of a long lane on the bank of Ted's Creek. The lane continued past the creek, but there was no bridge, so vehicles could go no farther. His place was thus very isolated deep in the woods west of Rough Edge. The massive oak, hickory, beech, and gum trees, interspersed with an occasional small field, provided excellent habitat for all kinds of wildlife. Nephews, brothers, in-laws, and friends over the years began to gravitate to the old man's place in the fall and winter to go hunting.

The number of hunters grew until one weekend each year was set aside for a community-wide hunt and cookout. Edwin, a nephew, had served in the army in World War II. Mr. Sullivan, one of his army buddies, for several years came all the way from Caspar to participate in this affair. Saturday was the day of the hunt, and that hunt lasted from sunup to sundown. Those participants knew to take with them into the woods a lunch and some snacks because one deer drive lasted from the time the hunters were placed on their stands until noon, and the second drive lasted from one o'clock until dusk. For safety purposes, all the hunters knew not to leave their stands. Such a large area was covered by each hunt that several hours might pass before a hunter even heard one of the hounds bark. The hours on the stand could become long and boring.

One man, a nephew's friend from Mobile, was a totally inexperienced hunter. He did not know the dos and don'ts of deer hunting. Being on a stand for hours without even hearing a bird chirp, the man grew restless, bored, and hungry. He leaned his shotgun against one of the huge hickory trees, fished around in his lunch sack, and got out a bag of potato chips. Placing the sack by his gun, he opened the bag of potato chips and reached in to help himself to a snack. Upon hearing a slight rustle of leaves, he looked up to see a huge eight-point buck standing there looking at him. Of course, by the time he dropped the potato chip bag and grabbed his shotgun, the buck had gone on his merry way.

Telling the story to the other hunters gathered around a campfire that evening, he said, "I was standing there with my hand in a potato chip bag when I looked up and saw that buck."

All the hunters had a good laugh at the expense of the Mobile man. Then the men around the fire turned their attention to the next day's cookout.

A feast it was, with every hunter bringing one or two dishes, plenty of iced tea, and a whole deer barbecued over a pit of red coals.

The Elder Statesman called the hunters to order when the dinner was ready and said, "Gentlemen, in the future if you come to hunt, don't get caught with your hand in a potato chip bag." Then he asked Rudy to offer thanks for the food.

Over the years, folks around Rough Edge began to use the expression, "Don't get caught with your hand in a potato chip bag," to cover any situation when a person might be taken by surprise.

Enough to Make a Grown Man Cry

The Elder Statesman and Fred developed a meticulous plan for a fishing expedition to Lake Martin. They left Rough Edge at three o'clock in the morning in order to be on the lake by seven. In tow was the old man's boat, into which fishing gear, coolers, ice, lunches, and bait were carefully stored.

The trip went smoothly all the way to the lake. The old man backed the boat trailer up to the top of the loading ramp, and Fred got out to untie the boat so it would float when the trailer was backed into the water. Fred managed to show his adroitness when he got tangled up with one of the tie-down straps. He lost his balance and took off running down the ramp, unable to get his feet back under him until just before hitting the water.

The Elder Statesman said, "Fred, as fast as you were running down that ramp, you had enough speed generated to run on the water halfway across Lake Martin. You were lucky to regain your balance."

Without further ado, they launched the boat and headed out into the lake. After coming upon a likely spot, they dropped anchor and commenced fishing. Fred was a sidearm caster. Each time he threw his line out, the baited hook came uncomfortably close to the Elder Statesman.

"Throw that thing overhanded!" commanded the old man. "You are going to hook me."

For a while Fred did throw overhanded, but with the excitement of catching fish, he relapsed. Fred's hook caught the Elder Statesman right on the bony spot behind his ear. It did not sink in because of the bone, but it cut a gash about an inch and a half long. The jerk on the line snapped it, and bait and hook went sailing out into the lake. Fred looked around, wondering what happened. The Elder Statesman showed Fred the gash while berating him severely for his careless method of casting. Upon opening the first aid kit, Fred got the antiseptic and Band-Aids out. In a few minutes, he had the wound neatly bandaged. The rest of the day on the water was uneventful.

On the way home, they stopped at a service station for gas and to stretch their legs. After returning to the pickup, the Elder Statesman turned the key but nothing happened.

"It's that loose connection on the battery," said the old man. "Get out, raise the hood, and wiggle the battery cable," he directed Fred.

Fred got out, raised the hood, and wiggled the battery cable. The Elder Statesman held the key in the start position, and when the cable and battery made contact, the truck fired up. Fred slammed the hood down but remained standing in front of the truck with a pained expression on his face.

"Come on. Let's go," the old man yelled out the window to Fred.

"I can't unless you come help me!" screamed Fred.

Being a rather rotund and short gentleman, when Fred had slammed the hood down, it had caught the midsection of his anatomy. Unfortunately, the hood had gone down far enough for the safety latch to catch. Fred could not raise the hood to free himself. Assessing the situation, the Elder Statesman realized that the only way to release Fred was to mash the hood down far enough to unlock the safety latch. Fred pulled up his shirt, revealing a deep purple bruise all the way across his midsection.

With tears welling up in his eyes, Fred sobbed, "That's enough to make a grown man cry."

Gina

rnold was not his usual self that morning. After spotting the trailer for the Elder Statesman, he came into the office a bleary-eyed, exhausted man. As he sat down in one of the chairs, Arnold's demeanor was so markedly different that the old man asked, "What's the matter with you, Arnold?"

Arnold said, "Coy and Betty came over to Rough Edge yesterday afternoon to see us. After an hour, they were getting ready to go home when Gina, their six-year-old daughter, put in to spend the night with us. Miriam agreed to let her stay. I knew that was a bad idea, but Miriam made it into a done deal.

"Everything was lovely until bedtime arrived. Gina began to sniffle and wanted to go home. We endured the crying kid until eleven o'clock. Since nothing we did comforted her, we decided to take her home to Falling Waters."

Arnold and Miriam had set out for Falling Waters at eleven-thirty, and about forty-five minutes later, they pulled up in front of the house. Arnold opened the car door and started to get out. Then Gina said, "We don't live here anymore."

"What!" shouted Arnold. "Why didn't you tell us that before we drove all the way over here? Where did you move to?" he demanded.

"We moved back to Brocton," whispered Gail.

A much-frustrated Arnold had gotten back into the car and driven another thirty miles to the house in Brocton, arriving there shortly after one o'clock in the morning. Arnold went to the door and knocked rather loudly several times, trying to awaken Coy and Betty, but without success.

When he returned to the car and got in, Gina told him, "They sleep upstairs."

That's why I couldn't wake them up, Arnold had thought. Noticing a ladder leaning against the house, Arnold got back out and placed it under the upstairs bedroom window. After climbing the ladder, he reached the window and began beating loudly on it. The racket woke a neighbor across the street. The neighbor, upon seeing a man on the ladder pounding on the window, thought he was trying to break into the house. Suspecting the worst, the neighbor called the law. The law arrived on the scene a few minutes later, demanding an explanation from a much-disgruntled Arnold.

The neighbor came out and listened to Arnold relate to the officer the events that had up to the episode with the ladder. When the neighbor heard Arnold mention Coy and Betty, he said, "They aren't at home. They have gone fishing on the Chickasawhay River tonight and will not be back until sometime in the morning."

There was nothing to do but take Gina back home with them. They had gotten back to Rough Edge around 3:00 a.m.

"I'm not going to bed," Arnold had said. "I have to get up and go to work at four o'clock, so it's no use."

The Elder Statesman listened to Arnold's story, laughing all the while.

"I will tell you this," said Arnold most forcefully. "Gina will never spend the night at my house again."

God Laughed

This excerpt from the life of the Elder Statesman exemplifies the fact that God does indeed have a sense of humor. He created man and woman, established the institution of marriage, and has laughed ever since. You see, men have certain strong points in their characters and personalities as well as weak points. Women have the same features in their makeups. What God intended was for a woman's strong points to exactly coincide with a man's weak points and for a man's strong points to coincide with a woman's weak points. Therefore, we find that between men and women, opposites attract so that a complete strong unit can be formed, with husbands and wives complementing each other.

Many times, that attraction results in a wedding. God looks down and sanctions the wedding and then says, "Figure it out." It's the figuring it out that generates all the sparks and fireworks. But isn't that the spice that keeps marriage from being dull and monotonous? Here are but a few examples.

The Elder Statesman's favorite food happened to be fish. Tuna, salmon, trout, bream, bass, catfish, and sardines are delicious to him, while his wife liked pork, liver, and onions. Bright, gay colors with plenty of flowers and plaids decorated her clothes, while he chose plain, conservative colors. When making a salad, he would combine lettuce, olives, raisins, sunflower seeds, and cheese, but she would use the little ears of pickled corn, brussels sprouts, and pickles over a little lettuce. She was a people person, while he did not like crowds and was more of a loner. She liked to be on the go, but he wanted to stay at home. The list could go on and on. After several years of marriage, one of those differences erupted one Saturday morning.

The Elder Statesman was a saver. Even back in his childhood and teen years, he saved money if he happened to get hold of any. His father paid him a quarter to shave him. Over time, that tightwad saved enough to buy himself a twenty-two rifle and a lawnmower. Now, his wife never had much money growing up. If she got any, she spent it. Therefore, a spender she became.

That Saturday morning, they entered into a discussion about the family finances with diverging points of view. As the discussion progressed, the divergence widened. It may also be said that the volume of their voices increased dramatically. Frustrated that no agreement was being reached, the Elder Statesman declared, "When they designed the first brick, they used your head to see how hard to make it."

"Yes," she retorted. "But they used yours to get it square."

Momentarily they both looked toward heaven and laughed right along with God.

Great Was the Fall

From the window of room 212-C in Helms Hall, the Elder Statesman had a superb view of students rushing around the campus. Right outside the window stood an ancient hackberry tree with an unusually large girth. One foggy morning while preparing to go to class, the Elder Statesman caught sight of a squirrel running toward the hackberry tree along a telephone cable suspended above the street. In the weeks that followed, he began to look for the squirrel. Many of those mornings he saw the squirrel running along the cable and jumping to a limb extending out from the tree. The squirrel never ran across the street, the Elder Statesman assumed, for fear of being run over by a vehicle.

Apparently, the full moon in October drove some students to become pranksters. During those days, some of the more immature students conducted panty raids; some painted the neck of the bust of Stephen D. Lee, the founder of the university, red; and some rolled places around the campus with toilet tissue. The ancient hackberry got a massive quantity of tissue.

It must be declared that the squirrel was delighted to have his favorite tree so well decorated with tissue. October was a dry month in East Point, its days cool, crisp, and clear. In those ideal conditions, the squirrel worked tirelessly for days on end constructing for himself a nest for the winter. He chose to use for the project that most abundant material, namely the toilet tissue. Before long, he had a large, beautiful white nest with a few leaves thrown in for good measure. The squirrel seemed proud of his handiwork as he hopped around on the ground, gathering his winter food supply.

Then, in the middle of November, there came one of those soaking, quite heavy at times, all-day rains. Alas, the squirrel's nest fell, and great was the fall of it. The next morning in total panic, the squirrel hopped from limb to limb all over the tree, surveying the collapse from every angle. The Elder Statesman observed all the activity just outside his window. He noted that the squirrel at last seemed to conclude that nothing of his nest could be salvaged. It sat down upon a limb, pondering what to do. That poor squirrel looked as if he were going to apply for disaster relief funds.

"Hellwo"

The bottom line is a mesmerizing entity that has caused highly intelligent, well-educated people to pace office floors, repeatedly sharpen pencils, scribble figures on reams of paper, and endure many sleepless nights. The goal of all these activities is always the same: to reduce the cost a business must bear to produce its goods and services.

The plant at which the Elder Statesman worked had a managerial group severely infected with inflamed bottom line mesmerism. One decision based upon their research and calculations was to use temporary employees during times of peak demand to perform many of the clerical duties inherent in the business. In slack periods, these temps could be laid off, leaving the plant with sufficient manpower without being overstaffed.

Brenda, the wife of a county politician, was hired as an inventory clerk in the traffic department's Brighteners Division. It was her job to keep up with the pounds of goods received from the production unit, the pounds of goods shipped, and the balance left over, which constituted the inventory on hand. The books were checked once a month, and they had to balance or the traffic foreman had to have a plausible explanation for any discrepancy.

Terry, the traffic foreman in Brighteners, called Brenda to check the figures for the month of July. Brenda had a speech impediment that caused her to say "hellwo" instead of "hello" when answering the telephone.

"Hellwo," she said when she answered Terry's call.

For several minutes, they went over the numbers, product by product, until they came to Brightener K, which made up two-thirds of all the material Terry handled.

Terry asked, "What are you showing in inventory?"

Brenda replied, "That one is too hard! I'm working on something else."

Having made the call from the Elder Statesman's office, Terry croaked to the old man, "That beats all I ever heard! I asked Brenda about Brightener K, and she said it was too hard, so she was working on something else!"

They struggled through the last two months of Brenda's summertime employment. Things settled down to normal after she left.

Terry often came to the Elder Statesman's office at break time for a cup of coffee. One day the phone rang while Terry was there. Gene asked to speak to Terry. "Someone called my office looking for you and left this number for you to call," Gene told Terry and hung up.

The unsuspecting Terry dialed the number, and a soft feminine voice said, "Hellwo."

A blanched, speechless Terry slowly hung up the phone. "That Gene! I'll kill him when I see him," screeched Terry as his face turned purple. "He found out that Brenda was working as a secretary in the analytical lab this summer and he gave me her number to call. I knew who it was when she said, 'Hellwo.'" The enraged Terry didn't cool off the rest of that day.

Highway 17

T he sudden appearance of the rare and unusual attracts our attention magnetically. Back in the ancient history of his life, the Elder Statesman attended M—— State University. The 189-mile distance from Rough Edge to the campus made it necessary for students to ride together to and from home and school. The Elder Statesman and his cousin rode with two young chaps from Butler, Ronald and Dan. Those trips were infused with quite a few adventures.

One of those events occurred in Greenfield. The cousin had been given a new car by his parents when he started college. He was known to exceed the legal limit imposed on the forward motion of vehicles on the public highways. On one such occasion, he was so engaged as he approached the railroad crossing in Greenfield. Now that crossing was higher in elevation than Highway 17, creating a requisite upward slant in the road approaching the tracks from either direction. The slant of the road and the high speed launched the car over the tracks. Having no wings, the car returned to the surface of the earth about fifty feet beyond the tracks. The racing car and the racing heartbeats of the passengers were practically indistinguishable.

Later trips provided other memorable events.

The Elder Statesman and his cousin, as well as the students from Butler, squeezed the very most time possible out of their weekend trips home. It was already dark when the Elder Statesman stopped in Butler to pick up Ronald and Dan one night. Proceeding north on Highway 15, they came to a place where the road went over a hill, only to descend sharply on the other side. As it descended, the road went around the shoulder of a hill such that there was a hill to the left and a drop-off to the right. Cut out of the hill to the left was a space for a roadside table with benches made of concrete.

"What in the world is going on up ahead?" Dan cried as the car climbed up the south side of the hill.

Lights were shining up into the trees above the roadside table. Not knowing what they were about to encounter, the Elder Statesman slowed the car as they passed over the crest of the hill. There before them was a car with one of the back wheels over the shoulder of the road where the drop-off began. That position caused the headlights to point up into the trees on the opposite side of the highway. The wheel over the shoulder was situated such that the car could not pull back up onto the road. The young men stopped by the roadside table and got out to see what was wrong. A young African American decked out in a suit, tie, white shirt, and highly shined black shoes got out and explained the situation.

"We were going to turn around here at the roadside table where we had enough room and go back to Butler. When we backed up, one of the back wheels dropped over the shoulder of the road and we could not get the car back on the road."

While they were talking, the driver, who was somewhat inebriated, backed up a little more, trying to get a running start to get back onto the road. That resulted in getting one of the front wheels off the shoulder. The car now had its two left wheels over the shoulder of the road, and it was sitting at about a forty-five-degree angle.

The driver decided to get out and join them up on the road. When he opened the door, he fell out of the car. They could hear him thrashing about as he rolled down the embankment all the way down to the muddy water-filled ditch some forty feet below. There was a loud splash followed by several minutes of scuffling as the driver slowly climbed back up to the road. It was a comical sight to see such a well-dressed young man smeared with a white limey goo.

Ronald knew one of them, a watch repairman from Butler, and offered to take them back to town. "No thanks. Someone will come along in a pickup and pull us back up on the road," the watch repairman courteously replied.

"Good luck! We have a long way to go tonight," Dan said out the window as the Elder Statesman pulled out and headed north up Highway 17.

I'll Be Watching You

Grandparents are typically overly indulgent toward their grandchildren, and the Elder Statesman and Diamond Lil were no exception. Their two granddaughters frequently came to visit them and pled for a trip to the Blue Bird Café, one of their favorite watering holes. Surrendering to their pleas and anxious looks, the old man and Diamond Lil loaded them into the car and drove the eight miles to the café. It happened to be in mid-July of the year that the girls were five and nine years old.

Business was rather brisk at the café that Saturday. Twenty-five or so patrons were enjoying their dinners while conversing in low tones with friends. The old man, Diamond Lil, and the granddaughters seated themselves at the vacant table near the cash register. The Elder Statesman glanced around the restaurant and nodded at the diners he happened to know. Carl, a gentleman from Vimco with silver white hair that covered his head and had grown into a beard that reached down to the middle of his chest—and who often played Santa Claus at stores in Jackson and Mobile—was dining in the Blue Bird Café that day.

Sarah, the five-year-old granddaughter, had a voice with tonal qualities that could be heard above the low murmur going on in the café. Her voice really projected itself when she was excited. The Elder Statesman, Diamond Lil, and the kids were about half-finished with their dinner when Carl, dressed in short pants, a matching shirt, and white suspenders, approached the cash register to pay for his meal.

The Elder Statesman leaned over and whispered to Sarah, "That is Santa Claus in his summer uniform."

Sarah excitedly jerked her head around and, looking at Carl with wide eyes, said loudly, "Linda, that is Santa Claus, and he is watching me!"

Many of the patrons, including Carl, heard Sarah and looked at her, smiling. After paying his bill, Carl walked over to Sarah and said, "Young lady, if you are a good girl, I will see you at Christmas! Just remember, I'll be watching you!"

An excited, breathless, speechless, awe-struck Sarah with wide-open mouth could only turn and stare at the Elder Statesman and Diamond Lil.

Impaired Judgement

Tipsy Tommy was the appellation by which he was known. In his younger days, he was a very good baseball player. When he was about eighteen years of age, he tried out for one of the professional teams. The coaches told him that he pitched with major league speed but that he needed to go home for about a year and develop better control. Tommy was much disillusioned. He came home and turned to booze. Eventually, he got a job at one of the local plants and after some years wound up in the Elder Statesman's crew. In that interval of years, his weight dropped from 190 pounds to 118 pounds. Of course, the constant imbibing impaired his judgment.

Hurricane Fredrick came upon the scene. Reasonable thought dictated that people should take every foreseeable precaution to avoid the danger Fredrick posed. However, Tommy deemed it safe to ride the storm out in his mobile home. In the middle of the night, when the storm was at its peak, Tommy's mobile home was shaking and rocking like it was about to be blown away. That was when Tommy decided to open the door and look out at what was happening. His home had a door that opened to the inside and a storm door that opened to the outside. Tommy opened the inside door with no problem, but when he barely cracked the storm door to the outside, the raging wind caught it, snatched it out of his hand, and ripped it off his home, taking it away, never to be seen again.

The week after the storm, Tipsy returned to work. One morning, he came into the Elder Statesman's office walking very gingerly.

"What's the matter with you?" asked the old man.

Tipsy said something unintelligible while looking down at the floor. Now Tipsy was a gentleman of African descent, and that morning, he came to work dressed in black.

"He's not going to tell you," said one of the other men who lived in his neighborhood, "but I will. This morning there was a heavy fog where we live. Tipsy came out of his house dressed in black and walked out to the street to wait for his ride. While waiting, a car came by and cut short the corner where Tipsy was standing. The driver did not see the African American dressed in black standing on the corner this foggy morning. Alas, he ran over both of Tipsy Tommy's feet. That is why he is walking so stiffly."

Impetuous, That He Is!

"Impetuous, by golly! That's what Houston is! Impetuous!" roared Joe Beach. "A few days ago we were deer hunting out in the piney woods. I had put the hunters on their stands. We were waiting for Doc to turn the dogs loose and begin the drive. One of the dogs barked, and immediately I heard a crashing sound out in the woods in front of me. I raised my gun in anticipation of seeing a fine buck. Lo and behold, Houston had left his stand and was tearing through the woods, stomping down pine saplings twelve feet tall, trying to head off the dogs!" Joe, his eyes still flashing in anger, related to the Elder Statesman. "I yelled at Houston, and he stopped."

"You are going to get someone shot leaving your stand like that. Stay here with me until the drive is over," Joe had commanded. The hunters gathered up after the drive was over to plan the next hunt. Unanimously, they had agreed to take Houston back to Rough Edge before some hunter got shot. His impetuousness made him an accident waiting to happen.

Sometime after that, the Elder Statesman's uncle was building his house. Houston, full of nervous energy, drove up to see the progress being made on it. At the time, a white particle board with a finish like ceramic tile was being glued to the kitchen walls up to a height of four feet. The adhesive being used to stick the particle board to the wall was very thick and tarlike. A serrated trowel was used to spread the adhesive in beads over the back of the board. Once the adhesive became tacky, the board was pressed against the wall, where it stuck in place.

The ever-impetuous Houston cried, "You don't need that trowel! That thing just gets in the way." Reaching into the bucket with his bare hand and retrieving a glob of adhesive, he said, "It's a lot faster spreading it with your hand."

He commenced spreading the goo over the next piece of particle board. Much to Houston's chagrin, when he finished smearing it and tried to clean his hands, nothing would remove the adhesive. The Elder Statesman's aunt gave Houston two sheets of newspaper with which he held the steering wheel of his car to keep from getting the adhesive on it. The Elder Statesman shook his head in amazement as Houston left with the newspaper now firmly glued to his hands.

"I wonder if that man ever read the directions on anything," Elder Statesman said as Houston's car disappeared from view. "Yep! Impetuous. That he is!"

Jim

W.J. was the pastor of the church the Elder Statesman attended. He excelled in preaching timely, effective sermons. Some were quite fiery, while others were tender and compassionate. An extrovert who knew how to mix and mingle with the members, he fell into their activities, be it work, fishing, hunting, or gardening. He and his wife had no children of their own, but they adopted a newborn baby boy, Jim. As years passed, it became apparent that Jim was a little slower than most children. He had the capacity to learn, but at his own pace.

W.J. realized that most likely Jim would be dependent on him for as long as he lived. Consequently, he began to teach him carpentry, since that was his own bivocational work. The church building needed some repairs and painting, so W.J. was on a stepladder outside, holding on to the window frame, calling for Jim to let the window down so he could paint it. The dry paint had the window stuck. W.J. soon became frustrated and began to yell at Jim to let the window down. In response, Jim caught the top of the window and put all his weight on it. The dry paint broke loose, allowing the window to descend with considerable force. W.J. had failed to notice that his grip on the window frame placed his fingers in the path of the descending window.

After an initial scream, W.J. could be heard pleading, "Let it up, Jim! Let it up!" over and over until Jim got the window up. Work was suspended for a few days until W.J.'s throbbing, swollen fingers became functional again.

The Elder Statesman had built his wife, Lillian, a patio. He engaged W.J. and Jim to build the forms and pour a sidewalk from the front porch to the north entrance of the patio and a sidewalk from the back door to the south entrance. The day arrived for the pour, and the ready-mix company called at nine thirty in the morning, saying they were on their way with the cement.

W.J. sent Jim to unload some of the trash off the pickup so they would have room for the tools. Jim stayed gone for much longer than necessary to unload the trash, so W.J. began to call him. Getting no answer to his calls, he and the Elder Statesman walked down the hill to see what was wrong. Jim had backed the pickup down a slope covered with thick, dewy Bahia grass. The pickup would do nothing but spin on the wet grass. The Elder Statesman had to hook his truck to the stuck vehicle and pull it back onto the road.

When they got to the job site, the Elder Statesman chided Jim, "You are the only person I know that gets stuck on top of the hill!"

Just How Dumb Can We Be?

Hiram bought a tractor and hay baler from Mr. Miller in Stapleton, Mississippi. The tractor ran on butane, while the baler was powered by its own gasoline engine. They were excellent pieces of farm equipment. But like all things mechanical, they could develop problems.

After a decade of hard use, the engine on the baler knocked off in the middle of the hay season. This happened back in the day when farmers didn't call mechanics or take their machinery to a shop. They affected the repairs themselves. Hence, Hiram's son (Edwin) and grandson (Moe L.) set to work on the engine. Hay season was always in the scalding hot summertime, and there are no shade trees in a hay field. The two farmer-mechanics were having a right jolly old time sweating profusely over that most inactive engine.

"Let's go get the other tractor," Edwin suggested. "It has a pulley on its side. We can bring it out here, set it up, and run a belt from the pulley to the baler engine. Then we can restart the other tractor and spin the baler engine fast enough to start it."

The Elder Statesman had left Rough Edge, walking to Old Lock One on a route that took him by the hay field where the disabled baler engine stubbornly refused to show any sign of life. He walked over to the tractor and leaned against a rear tire, becoming a casual observer for several minutes. No matter how fast the sweating pair turned the engine with the belt, it only spit and sputtered.

Finally, the Elder Statesman asked, "Are you having trouble?"

Because of the heat and the engine problem, Moe L. roared for maximum effect with carefully selected profanity, "We can't get this **** **** engine to run. We have been out here in the sun for **** **** nearly two hours working on it."

"Well," said the Elder Statesman, "if you will put a twist in the belt and spin the engine, it will start up. Right now you are turning the engine backward."

Edwin and Moe L. looked at each other, wondering, *Just how dumb can we be?* One spin of the engine after they put a twist in the belt, and the engine roared to life.

Lawrence of Arabia and the Scrapyard Bike

S ymbiosis best describes the relationship between Terry the foreman and Francis the hourly hand. That is, most of the time. However, some occasions stretched that relationship past the point of civility.

Warehouse space became scarce because of the large volume of material produced. A decision was made to bring a man in on overtime Saturday to transfer much of that material to a warehouse belonging to another unit for storage until it was time to ship it to customers. Terry was the foreman that came in that day, and Francis was the forklift operator. The weather had turned bitterly cold during the night, so by work time, frozen puddles were everywhere. After several trips up and down the street on the forklift, Francis was chilled to the bone.

The company used a lot of rags in its operation, especially cleaning up minor spills and wiping off sample jars. The rags they purchased came packed in large cardboard boxes. Mainly they were torn or otherwise damaged hospital bed sheets and worn-out doctors' and nurses' uniforms. Francis went into the warehouse to the rag box, got four of those damaged sheets, and wrapped himself in them, leaving only his arms sticking out. He was trying by that means to keep warm while riding on his forklift.

Francis made several more trips up and down the street, the ends of the sheets flapping in the wind behind him. Finally, Terry looked out of the office window and did a double take when he saw Francis all decked out in his sheets.

"He looked like Lawrence of Arabia riding out across the desert sands," exclaimed Terry over the phone to the Elder Statesman.

Most of the shipping foremen had bicycles in the plant because they had to cover large areas. The company would not buy anymore new bicycles, but they would buy parts to maintain those that the foremen already had. Terry was one of the few that did not have a bicycle, but he hit upon a plan to get one. He located in the scrapyard an old discarded bicycle frame from which all the usable parts had been salvaged. Each week, he ordered a part to fit that bicycle frame. Over a few months, he gradually assembled a practically new bicycle. Terry was so proud of his bike when riding it around the plant.

One day he noticed that the front fender was rubbing against the tire. With his right foot, he kicked at the fender, intending to move it a little so that it would no longer rub on the tire. The only problem was he missed the fender and his foot went into the spokes, which carried his foot up to the forks into which the front wheel was mounted. The bike came to an abrupt stop, throwing Terry over the handlebars. He landed flat on his back on the concrete street, knocking the breath out of him. Stunned, he lay there for several minutes until he got his breath back.

The Elder Statesman was in Terry's office, enjoying a cup of coffee. Terry called Francis in and told him, "The chain has come off my bicycle. How about going out there and putting it back on for me?"

About twenty minutes later, Terry looked out of the office window and a look of panic crossed his countenance. Without a word, he sprang from his chair and charged out the door. In a minute, a much-disgusted Terry came back into the office.

"What's the matter?" asked the Elder Statesman.

"I thought Francis knew how to put a chain back on a bicycle. He went out there and took the pedals off and the large sprocket. To do so, he took out that middle section where the pedals are attached. Just as I got out there, I saw several ball bearings fall into the storm drain," cried Terry. With a sorrowful lament, Terry moaned. "And I've only had it back in operation for a month!"

Lazy Dogs and Bootleggers

I n the old days, Rough Edge met all the requirements to be classified as a frontier village. Under those conditions, bootlegging corn whiskey was looked upon by the local folks as an honorable but illegal profession. It was illegal because no tax was paid on the product when it was sold. The Elder Statesman gained a reputation for producing some of the finest white lighting in the county. Most of the old gentlemen in and around Rough Edge kept a jug hidden somewhere around their homes. In the winter, they would take a swallow or two before going to bed, claiming that it was the best medicine they had.

The Elder Statesman's still was located in a canebrake on the edge of a swamp behind his house. The only road to his place ended in his front yard, making access to his still by vehicle impossible. The old man recruited Randy Lane to help him whenever he was running off a batch of brew. Randy was not exactly of the right temperament to be a bootlegger, being a very nervous and easily excitable man. They had harvested a small field of corn, carried some of it to the still site, and made several barrels of mash, which were ready to be distilled.

Friday morning, they began the process. Shortly, a trickle of that liquid fire began flowing into a jug. The Elder Statesman sampled some of the stuff after it had cooled off just to be sure it met his standards for a high-quality product.

Randy rushed up to him all bug-eyed and excited, reporting, "I heard a car up at the house. Do you suppose it's the sheriff and his men?"

The Elder Statesman retorted, "I don't know, but I'll go up to the house and check it out. If you hear me yell, turn these barrels of mash over, tear up this still, and get out of here."

The Elder Statesman cautiously made his way up to the house. The old man always drew a line across the driveway when he was operating the still. If a vehicle came down the driveway, the tires would blot out part of that line, and he would know if anyone had been there. No car was parked in the front yard. Neither was any part of the line blotted out. The morning's activities had made the old man hungry. Thus, while at the house, he went into the kitchen and made himself and Randy each a sandwich.

The old man's dog was stretched out asleep on the front porch. When the Elder Statesman came out of the house, he stepped on that dog's tail. The ensuing howl could be heard a mile away. Down at the still, a jittery Randy supposed that the dog's howl was the old man yelling the prearranged alarm. In a minute or two, Randy had turned over all the barrels of mash and demolished the still with an ax before striking out through the woods.

When the Elder Statesman arrived at the still site and saw the wreckage, he thought Randy had seen the lawmen approaching on foot and so had destroyed the still. Therefore, the Elder Statesman took off slogging his way through the swamp.

A few days later, the Elder Statesman and Randy met up and pieced together what had happened Friday morning. Upon returning to the still to reconstruct it, they found Randy's five cell flashlight. His system had flooded with adrenaline when the dog howled and he had apparently squeezed that flashlight so tightly that he left the impression of his fingers on it.

The Elder Statesman, viewing the wrecked still, considered himself lucky that the law had not yet caught him. Then and there he ended his career as a bootlegger.

Lil's Conversion

The Elder Statesman's conversion of Lil, his wife, from a homebody to an outdoors woman proved to be such a monumental task that he could never fully affect it. No way would she exchange the comfort of air-conditioning for the natural atmosphere of the exterior.

The Elder Statesman really wanted an activity that he and Lil could enjoy participating in together. One of the trial balloons he floated was deer hunting. Lil had much to learn to become a competent hunter. She had to know how to handle a rifle rather than treating it as if she were allergic to it. She had to learn to be quiet, to be still, and to leave off all those good-smelling things women love to dab all over themselves. Success would provide them many hours of enjoyment together, regardless of whether they ever killed a deer.

Friday afternoon was set aside for their first hunt together. It turned out to be one of those chill-bump, teeth-chattering, cold, overcast days when a mist of tiny ice crystals floated gently in the air. They walked three-quarters of a mile to get to the place where the knuckle of a ridge dropped off sharply to a stream bottom—a place the Elder Statesman knew deer traveled through. When they arrived at the place, he took the time to rake all the leaves away from the base of two trees where they were going sit. Doing so eliminated all possibility of a movement creating noise. After sitting down and leaning back against the trees, they waited in anticipation of a deer passing along the stream bottom.

Experienced hunters know that the later it gets in the afternoon, the better the chance of seeing a deer. Just as the optimum time arrived, Lil got a tickle in her throat. Her eyes watered as she struggled to hold back a cough. Nature could not be overcome, and the blast of that cough lifted leaves off the ground fifteen feet away.

The Elder Statesman stood up, shouldered his rifle, and said, "Let's go. After that cough, there is no need to stay any longer."

Lil explained apologetically, noting the frustration in his attitude.

Converting Lil to an outdoors woman came crashing down, leaving a wreckage with no hope of repair. In all fairness, it must be said that when the effort at conversion ended, Lil experienced much relief. The passage of time revealed that dining out was an activity they enjoyed together without either one having to change a thing. The frustration of both parties was gone!

Loose Talk

Some patrons of verbosity elevate their glibness to an art form capable of inflicting upon those within range of their voice a severe case of audio exhaustion. Homer was a practitioner of that art. He loved to express his thoughts and opinions upon most any topic of conversation that happened to come up.

Bert, one of the traffic foremen, had a daughter engaged to Marty. Plans for the wedding were being finalized. A wedding cake, a wedding dress, reception refreshments, and decorations were all being selected by the daughter and her mother. Things were fairly well advanced when word of the event reached Homer. Learning that Marty was of a different ethnic group, Homer stated his opinion of the affair to the men gathered in Gene's office for lunch. Some of his remarks were blatantly unkind concerning the young people. Thomas, another traffic foreman, heard Homer's remarks and conceived a plan to teach him a lesson.

Thomas called Bert and related an account of Homer's remarks. He suggested that Bert enlist the Elder Statesman to call Homer pretending to be a lawyer and go after him hard and heavy. Bert and the Elder Statesman made their plan and called Gene's office the next day at lunch, asking to speak to Homer.

Being ever ready to talk, Homer took the phone from Gene and said, "Hello. This is Homer."

Thereupon the Elder Statesman, invoking a deep bass voice, said, "I'm Henry Field, an attorney representing Mr. Bert _____. He tells me that some of your adverse comments about his daughter's wedding have gotten back to Rough Edge and caused his daughter and Marty to break up. The wedding has been called off on account of you. Now Bert is out the cost of a wedding cake, a wedding dress, rent for the place to have the reception, refreshments, and decorations, as well as the cost of the gowns for the ladies and tuxedos for the men in the wedding party. Also, there will be punitive charges for the damage your comments have done to his daughter. Homer, unless I hear from Bert that you and he have come to a settlement, I will be filing a suit against you on his behalf to collect for the expenses he incurred and for the damages your talk has caused. I shall see you in court on May 16. Goodbye, sir."

Hardly had the Elder Statesman hung up when the phone rang. Homer's panic was evident when he screamed, "Bert! What's going on? I just got a call from a lawyer saying that you were going to sue me."

"That's right, Homer," said Bert. "All that loose talk that you have been doing about my daughter and Marty got back to Rough Edge, causing them to break up. All that money I spent on her wedding is gone. You know that new house that you built? I am going to be living in it when my lawyer gets through with you. See you in court."

Bert casually hung up the phone to await developments. Less than five minutes later, the door of the office flew open, exposing a visibly shaken Homer.

Wide-eyed and pale, Homer pleaded, "Bert, what can we do?"

Unable to restrain himself any longer, Bert burst out laughing. Homer was a much-relieved and reformed man after Bert finally explained what they had done.

"I'm not talking about anybody else ever," swore Homer.

Mrs. Swaf

The entrepreneurial spirit survives in Rough Edge, but it does not flourish because the town's small population does not generate enough trade to support large enterprises. In fact, business establishments have declined until only one service station and store combination remains. Therefore, the Rough Edge folks must travel to other towns or cities to do their shopping.

Nancy, a neighbor of the Elder Statesman, in her shopping journeys located a fabric shop in Milton that she really liked. Nancy was a highly talented musician with a voice that ranged from bass to soprano and a tone that made listeners think they were hearing the angels sing. She was part of a trio of which Lil, the Elder Statesman's wife, was also a member. Through practice sessions and performances at church and social events, Lil and Nancy had become close friends.

As wives and mothers will do, if they find a shop most satisfying to their tastes, they share that discovery with their friends. Nancy was beaming as her descriptive narrative about the shop transported Lil into euphoric anticipation of strolling among bolts of cloth of all kinds and colors. Rounding out the great things about the shop was its well-stocked and wide variety of notions, which made it easy to match buttons, zippers, and thread with the cloth.

Nancy raved about Mrs. Swaf, the store owner. "She is so helpful," gushed Nancy. "She has a great eye for selecting the different fabrics to keep in stock. I can find patterns in styles that I like and that fit me. She has such a warm, outgoing personality that shoppers love her."

Three months later, Nancy, looking most perplexed, came to the Elder Statesman's house to chat with Lil. Being sensitive to her friend's unusual attitude, Lil declined to pry into her changed status, concluding that if Nancy wanted her to know, she would share the disturbance with her.

Nancy said, "I have never been so embarrassed in my life. I have been in the fabric shop in Milton many times. I always chat with Mrs. Swaf while selecting the material I want to buy. Friday, I was there looking at different materials when Mrs. Swaf walked up. I asked, 'How are you, Mrs. Swaf?' She replied, 'You have been in my shop many times in the last few years, and in our conversation, you always call me Mrs. Swaf, I assume because of the sign over the door. My name is not Mrs. Swaf. Those letters stand for Southwest Alabama Fabrics.'"

With a hint of red creeping up her neck to her cheeks and ears, Nancy said, "I could have gone through the floor. Just imagine, I had been calling the wonderful lady Mrs. Swaf for years."

Neighbors and Turnip Greens

The Elder Statesman had through the years maintained a charge account at the hardware in Churchwell. It was easier to get items he wanted, charge them, and write one check at the end of the month to pay for them. Saturday morning, he went to the hardware store to get some PVC pipe fittings and glue. The old man usually encountered someone he knew with whom he chatted about local events. Hunting, football, the weather, and politics were all analyzed as if they were nuclear physicists seeking a newly theorized subatomic particle.

It chanced to be at a moment when the ardent conversationalists were adjourning their gathering that a man walked in whose deeply tanned skin, ambling gait, and denim work clothes revealed him to be a farmer. He roamed around the store for a while. The Elder Statesman was casually observing him when a young female clerk approached him and asked, "Can I help you?"

"Oh, yes," said the farmer. "I want some turnip seeds."

"They are in the back. Come with me and I will get you fixed up."

The two walked away from the Elder Statesman, so he gazed around, looking for something else upon which to focus his attention. In a few minutes, the clerk returned to the counter near the old man, a perplexed expression having replaced her normal smile.

Not directing her comments to anyone in particular but rather speaking to the group of people standing around the counter, she declared in disgust, "I'm glad that man I just waited on is not my neighbor. He just bought twenty-nine cents worth of turnip seeds. That is about half of the smallest scoop we use to measure them. He is not planning on sharing turnips with anybody. I don't want anyone for a neighbor who will not even share turnips with me."

Never a Care

Diamond Lil occasionally exhibited a few attributes found only in the rarefied atmosphere of inattentiveness. In the early days of dating the Elder Statesman, they sometimes went to a drive-in movie in Grove Hill. Lil worked as a seamstress, and the Elder Statesman was in school at the university, so most of their dates were on the weekends. Lil grew up in Stapleton, Mississippi, which at the time was a very rural place. Having no television, her family went to bed shortly after dark, a habit Lil had practiced for many years, so much so that she became sleepy before nine o'clock.

The Elder Statesman still testifies to the fact: "One thing Lil has never seen are the words, 'The End,' when the movie is over. She is always asleep by that time."

Lil and the Elder Statesman departed the environs of Rough Edge to travel with Jane to various art events, sometimes to sign prints, sometimes to shows where Jane had entered a painting, and sometimes to see the work of other artists. After one such trip, they were traveling south from Memphis down Interstate 55. They left the interstate, going over to the Natchez Trace and continuing south. Being in no hurry, they stopped often to read the historical markers posted along the road. The fall colors beautified the roadside and woods with spectacular red, yellow, green, and brown leaves. Soon they crossed the Ross Barnett Reservoir just east of Jackson.

An hour later, the Elder Statesman, who was driving, asked, "How far is it to Morton?"

Lil looked at the map and replied, "About an inch."

In their travels, when the Elder Statesman grew tired or sleepy, Jane would take over the driving duties. Turning east onto Highway 82, they stopped to fuel up the car and change drivers. Jane took over the driving, and the Elder Statesman cautioned her to turn right when she came to Highway 45. In spite of the incessant chatter of Lil and Jane, the exhausted old man was soon fast asleep.

Two hours later, he woke up and asked, "Where are we?"

The two women, who were so engrossed in their bantering that they had never considered where they were, answered, "We don't know."

Just then, they passed a sign that read, "Two miles to Columbus." The wide-awake Elder Statesman sat bolt upright, exclaiming, "You missed the turn at Highway 45, taking us fifty miles out of the way! Thankfully, we can turn onto the Highway 45 East and rejoin the four-lane part of 45 at Crawford."

The two women never ceased chattering and never realized that they would have been in Tuscaloosa rather than Meridian if the old man had not woken. With never a care, how blissfully those two women traveled!

Never on a Friday

T he Elder Statesman read meters for a local power company for nearly ten years after he retired from a nearby chemical plant. The experiences of meter readers vary from the humorous to the sublime.

The Elder Statesman arose at four thirty in the morning in order to get ready for work, travel to Jefferson, gas up the company pickup he used, get his equipment, and be in Patterson by seven o'clock. Just west of the main intersection in Patterson, a road turned left and circled around by St. John's Church. Directly across the road from the church was a dead-end lane about a quarter mile long. Approximately forty residences lined both sides of the lane. The Elder Statesman always made sure to read the meters along the lane in the middle of the day and in the middle of the week because the people living in that area consumed a lot of strong drinks in the late evenings—especially Friday evenings—and there was one way in and one way out of the place.

On one occasion he noticed a large plastic mesh bin full of beer cans standing by the lane. Continuing down the lane, he read the last meter and turned around to exit the area. But someone had tipped the bin over, depositing a huge mound of beer cans in the road.

The Elder Statesman stopped at the pile, beside which a young man was standing, and said to him, "Do you want me to run over these cans?"

"Yes," replied the young man.

Forthwith, the old man plowed the pickup straight into the pile. It was a strange sight to see the pickup pushing down the road a pile of beer cans higher than the hood of the pickup. All the young man wanted was to get the cans crushed so they took up less space when he carried them to sell.

Not long afterward, the Patterson route was assigned to another meter reader who lived closer to the area. He was reading meters along that same lane one Friday afternoon when gunfire broke out. Being away from his truck, he had no choice but to make a run for it. He wound up lying facedown in a collard patch next to a rather rotund black lady.

Looking at him, the lady said, "Fellow, as soon as you can, you had better get out of here. If they will shoot me, a black woman, they will kill you!"

Her words were a source of great discomfort to him. He never did explain to the Elder Statesman how he extricated himself from that situation, but he did tell the old man that from then on, he heeded his advice and never went down that lane again in the evening, especially Friday evenings.

No More Tape

S arah, the Elder Statesman's granddaughter, chipped a small bone fragment off her pelvis when she fell while practicing volleyball at school. An examination by an orthopedic doctor in Mobile revealed the extent of the damage to be minor. However, the bone scan revealed something on the femur that should not have been there. The doctors thought they knew what showed up on the scan, but to be sure, Sarah was sent to Atlanta to a hospital associated with a university for tests. The doctors in Atlanta concurred with those in Mobile that the growth was a bone tumor. The best procedure for dealing with the tumor was an injection with a chemical that would freeze the growth, killing it.

A date was set for the procedure. As with any medical procedure, follow-up checks and limited physical activity were the order of the day. Sarah responded very well to the treatment, even though she was a small, young girl. The tiny incision for the camera used to guide the needle to the proper location was closed with tape.

After the requisite number of days, time came to remove the tape. I do not know the adhesive used on the tape, but it was strong enough to hold a hundred-car train together.

Sarah's mother tried to peel it off with no luck. Warm water did not weaken its grip. An attempt to soften the adhesive with a hair dryer proved futile. Finally, a crying Sarah endured her mother pulling the tape off while applying heat with the hair dryer. A very red patch of skin on Sarah's hip revealed where the tape had been. All was well until Sarah went to the bathroom. Lo, her underwear was stuck to her hip because of a coating of adhesive left behind by the tape. For the second time that day, Sarah suffered through the removal of the material stuck to her hip.

A lot of talk among family members centered on Sarah's procedure. She was fortunate to have accidentally chipped her pelvis, fortunate that the doctors in Mobile had spotted the irregularity in the bone scan, and fortunate to have had nearby doctors and a hospital that could provide her the best treatment.

One day while the family was talking about Sarah's experience, she chimed in, saying, "If I ever have another procedure, no more tape will be put on my butt!"

Things were back to normal in Rough Edge.

One Bad Day

A black cloud of gloom took up permanent residence over the head of Meese. He was jinxed beyond all statistical probability. Some of the dire events the Elder Statesman had been an eyewitness to, and some were related to him by Meese in graphic oral fashion.

Summertime was not Meese's favorite season, as he was a short but very muscular man who liked to work outside on his off days. Clouds of dust boiled up as he attacked with a rake the leaves, limbs, and trash that had collected in his yard. Though the hour was early, the expenditure of energy soon had Meese sweating profusely. The continuous vigorous application of the rake to the yard for more than two hours resulted in his shirt becoming drenched. However, the end of the project was now in sight.

Meese had a pile about four feet high and ten feet in diameter when he finished raking. Going to his shop, he filled a pint jar with gasoline from his gas can, returned to the pile, and poured the gas all over it. Reaching into his shirt pocket, he retrieved a box of matches and commenced to try to strike one. However, the match would not strike because the box had gotten damp in the sweat-drenched shirt pocket.

All the time he was trying to strike a match, the gas on the pile was vaporizing and spreading out over the yard. Finally, the match hit a dry spot on the box and ignited. Immediately there was a thunderous explosion! The huge pile of leaves and trash blasted all over the yard and Meese. His eyebrows were singed off, and the heat turned his exposed skin a bright red. Meese was propelled about ten feet backward and deposited on the ground flat of his back.

When telling this misadventure to the Elder Statesman, Meese said, "My neighbor across the road came running out of his house, thinking someone had wrecked in his yard."

Not long thereafter, the cloud of gloom rained on Meese again.

He and the Elder Statesman launched the old man's canoe into Bradley's Creek. They paddled upstream to the place where Red Creek ran into Bradley's Creek. Turning into Red Creek, they began fishing. A short distance up stream, they came upon a tree that had fallen across the creek. The tree was just high enough above the water that the canoe would go under it, but the men had to step over the tree and back into the canoe.

The Elder Statesman was in the front of the canoe, so he put the nose of the canoe under the tree. He then stepped over the tree and back into the canoe. He paddled the canoe forward until Meese could make the same move. The Elder Statesman looked up the creek and made a cast into the large clear pool in front of him.

Then he heard Meese cry, "You've gotta do something."

Looking back, he saw Meese bear-hugging the tree with his ankles in the canoe. His legs and torso were stretched inches above the water. There wasn't much the

Elder Statesman could do. It was a testimony to Meese's great strength that he somehow managed to pull that canoe backward to the point that he got his whole body back aboard without getting wet.

The Elder Statesman mused, "I guess your little cloud of gloom had a silver lining around it today!"

Panty Power

P oliticians are not the only ones to play politics. Within the ranks of the industrial world's personnel, ambitious souls continuously strive to advance themselves by any and all means possible. The Elder Statesman and Big Boy observed such maneuvering at the plant where they worked as traffic foremen.

Management contracted with a personnel agency to supply people to perform some of the record keeping and other less demanding functions of the production units. Lois was assigned to the same area as Big Boy. It did not take Lois long to discover that a flirtatious attitude aimed at the production engineer allowed her to shift anything she did not want to do off onto Big Boy. He was left with no means to redress the grievances inflicted on him by Lois. It was especially galling that a noncompany person could have him, a company man, forced to do her work.

A hazardous materials training session was scheduled to begin one Thursday morning out in the pavilion. It lasted all day, with drinks and dinner provided by the company. All the company personnel assigned to units handling hazardous materials were required to attend. Approximately seventy-five people met for the class and seated themselves in nine rows of steel folding chairs. The traffic foremen, including the Elder Statesman and Big Boy, sat near the back of the room, while the production engineer was in the front row with Lois sitting by his side.

Bob, observing the relative positions of Big Boy and Lois, asked Big Boy, "Why aren't you sitting up there by the boss instead of Lois?"

A grimace spread over Big Boy's face when the Elder Statesman chimed in, "Bob, you know Big Boy can't overcome panty power."

From then on, Panty Power became Lois's nickname among the traffic foreman. Every time Big Boy complained about the things he had to do that really were Lois's job, the other foremen reminded him, "You can't overcome Panty Power."

Pig's Peaches

P ig, the appellation of that huge man, was indicative of his massive physique. Advancing south from Chilton County with his pickup loaded with peaches, he entered Rough Edge around ten in the morning. Pig stopped by the Elder Statesman's abode, seeking directions to Churchwell and also to sell some of his peaches. The two youngest teenage sons of the Elder Statesman were the only ones home when Pig arrived. Having no money, they could not buy any peaches, but they did give him directions to Churchwell.

"Turn off Highway 24 at the top of the hill. In about four miles, you will come to the road from Benton to Churchwell. Take a left, and in six more miles, you will arrive in Churchwell."

Pig thanked them and left for Churchwell. When he was out of sight, the older brother said, "Come on and let's go get some peaches."

"Where and with what are we going to get peaches?" inquired the younger brother.

"Just come on and you'll see," said the older one.

Grabbing a sack, they took off on foot in pursuit of Pig. The older brother had noticed that Pig had opened a few of the cases of peaches for display. He, therefore, had directed Pig to Churchwell over some very bumpy dirt roads. As Pig made his way to Churchwell over those roads, quite a few peaches bounced out of the open cases and fell to the road. The two brothers walked along that road and picked up a sack full of peaches.

Pig was a jovial sort of individual. The next time he came to Rough Edge, he stopped by the Elder Statesman's place and joked with the brothers about the trick they had pulled on him. They became such good friends that Pig often came down to spend a few days and hunt with them.

It was on one of those trips that Pig related an unusual adventure he had earlier that year.

"As you can see, I am a pretty hefty individual. One day during my travels peddling peaches, I stopped at a country store for some refreshments. Having procured the items I wanted, I got back into my pickup and fastened my seat belt. Being as large as I am, my midsection reached all the way out to the steering wheel. I did not notice when I fastened the seat belt that I had run it through the steering wheel. Everything was lovely as I pulled away from the store. In a little way, I came to a curve in the road. When I tried to steer the truck around the curve, the seat belt prevented me from turning the steering wheel. It was a short but exciting ride down into the woods!"

They refilled Pig's coffee cup and waited anxiously for another story.

Probing Problems in Proctology

The Elder Statesman had the great misfortune to develop a severe case of hemorrhoids from which he suffered for a number of years. Finally, when the discomfort became unbearable, he went to see a proctologist in Mobile.

The day of the appointment arrived, and with nervous dread, the Elder Statesman entered the doctor's office, registered with the receptionist, and breaking out in a cold sweat, took a seat in the waiting room. Looking around at the singular countenance of dread on all the other patients' faces raised his apprehension to stratospheric levels. Just then, a lady reentered the waiting room after being examined, staggered over to a chair, and as best as she could, lowered herself into it.

"Oh, he killed me. He killed me," she continuously moaned while waiting for her husband to pay for the visit.

Under the influence of the moaning, the Elder Statesman sat gripping the arms of his chair with white-knuckled fingers. As he was about to make a break for the door, a nurse with a clipboard full of papers called him to come back to the examination room. There was no escape!

Forget modesty! When being examined for hemorrhoids, it does not exist. The Elder Statesman was given one of those new-and-improved hospital gowns, which had a superb ventilation system, and was told to remove his clothes, put on the gown, and lay facedown on the examination table. When that feat was accomplished, the doctor strolled into the room and casually walked over to the Elder Statesman.

A nurse untied the straps holding the back of his gown together. She folded it neatly out of the way, exposing the area in question to view. The doctor stepped on a foot pedal, and the examination table folded upward in the middle, bringing the Elder Statesman's posterior to the proper level for examination.

When the doctor slapped a handful of cold lubricating gel over the exposed orifice, the patient exclaimed, "I've had it now!"

The doctor reached over to a tray and picked up an instrument of torture called a proctor scope. As he began to insert the scope into the offending orifice, he said to the twitching patient, "Just relax."

"How can I relax?" cried the Elder Statesman. "You are probing around in the place where every nerve in my body is tied together!"

The exam was soon complete. The patient removed the flapping gown, cleaned off the excess lubricating gel, and dressed. It was with a rather stiff gait that the patient stumbled to a chair in the waiting room and eased himself down to the seat. For about fifteen minutes, he sat trying to catch his breath.

Having made the necessary arrangements, his wife came over, took him by the arm, and announced, "You are scheduled for surgery next Thursday."

The following week, the Elder Statesman checked into the hospital, was given another well-ventilated gown, and was put to bed. Soon a nurse came in with a glass full of fleet, which he had to drink. That potent laxative worked its magic. The patient spent the entire night going to the bathroom. A huge orderly shook the bleary-eyed patient awake at 8:00 a.m.

Carting in another instrument of torture with which to give him an enema, the orderly said, "They call me the rear admiral, and I've got to see spring water."

"I've been up and down all night going to the bathroom," lamented the patient.

Hardly had the rear admiral left the room when a nurse came in with a gurney. "I'm taking you down for presurgery testing," she stated briskly. They reran all the tests done the week before during his office visit, plus a few others.

The Elder Statesman bemoaned in a woeful voice, "I'm so sore that I can't stand to be touched with a powder puff."

Dinner, served soon after he returned to his room, lifted his spirits a little. That is, until five o'clock when a nurse came in bearing the glad tidings, "Here's another glass of fleet that you have to drink."

"What?" shouted the patient. "Why didn't you tell me that earlier? I wouldn't have eaten anything. Now I'll spend another night going to the bathroom."

"Sorry about that, but you are scheduled for surgery at eight o'clock in the morning."

After two nights with little sleep, the Elder Statesman was woken again by the rear admiral. "I've got to see more spring water," he announced.

By now the patient felt as though he had been sandpapered and immersed in alcohol. As the enema progressed, beads of sweat the size of buckshot popped out on his forehead. Fortunately, nurses with a gurney soon took him to the operating room. A saddle block injection relieved his pain but left him fully awake. Shortly after, the doctors came in and the surgery began. As they worked on the patient, they were laughing and talking about duck hunting in the Mobile River Delta.

Looking over his shoulder, the Elder Statesman cried, "Hey, let's get serious back there! This is me that you are cutting on." He turned his head back around and spied a pretty young nurse stationed at the head of the operating table.

When he later related the story, the Elder Statesman would chuckle. "I was flirting with the nurse all the while the doctors were slinging chitterlings into a bucket behind me."

When the surgery was over, the patient was taken to the recovery room. Other patients there were moaning and crying and praying. After a few minutes of listening to that racket, the Elder Statesman buzzed for the nurse.

She came to his bed and asked, "Yes? What can I do for you?"

The Elder Statesman roared, "This racket is driving me crazy! Take me to my room."

"I'll have to see if the doctor says it's OK," she replied and left to find the doctor.

When she returned some thirty minutes later, the deadening effect of the saddle block had worn off, and the Elder Statesman was leading the prayer meeting. The doctor allowed him to return to his room, so the nurses wheeled him out of recovery, down the hall, and into his room.

It was a rough ride. The jarring created when the gurney wheels ran over the threshold of his room shot searing pain through his nether region. The trip seemed to last an eternity, but finally they got him arranged in bed.

Of course, he eventually had to go through the entire process to be sure everything worked properly. The time came for that first post-op trip to the bathroom. The Elder Statesman screamed loudly enough to wake half the city. "It was as if there were a protruding piece of barbed wire that someone grabbed and gave a yank," he would later say.

He barely made it to the bed, where he collapsed, a sobbing, moaning wreck. His wife was like Job's friend, a poor comforter. "If you think this is painful, you should have a baby," she said several times that day and for several days afterward.

One week after his release from the hospital, the Elder Statesman returned to the doctor's office for his first post-op checkup. In the waiting room, there was a lady who had also had hemorrhoid surgery.

With his wife sitting by him, the Elder Statesman inquired of that lady, "Do you have any children?'

"Oh yes, I have four," she answered.

"Which was the worst: having a baby or having hemorrhoid surgery?" he asked.

"I would have all four children at the same time before I would have this surgery again!" she vowed.

The Elder Statesman quipped, "I would buy a little red wagon and haul them around behind me before I would go through this again."

The lady laughed and nodded in agreement with him.

Retribution. How Swift!

The Elder Statesman was thunderstruck by the revelation the lady at the cash register made to him. He, his daughter, and her friend were on their way from Rough Edge to Stonewall to see the State versus Alabama football game. York, Alabama, was halfway between the two places, so around eleven o'clock, they stopped there to get a bite to eat. As he was paying for their lunch, the old man casually mentioned to the lady at the cash register where they were going.

She said, "You had better hurry. I just saw on TV that the game has been moved up an hour and a half so it can be televised. It is going to start at one o'clock rather than two thirty."

The Elder Statesman left York, depressing the fuel control pedal to the greatest extent possible without attracting and incurring the wrath of the gentlemen with the flashing blue lights. Good fortune smiled on them when they arrived on campus. A student backed out of a parking space in front of a dorm near the stadium. Leaving the car in that space, they walked to the stadium and were climbing the spiral stairs up to their seats when Alabama received the opening kickoff.

Things went smoothly the first quarter, with the girls enjoying every minute of their first trip to a college football game. They didn't even notice that they were getting blistered by the hot October sun.

In the second quarter, the optical focus of the Elder Statesman centered on the lateral walkway halfway up the stadium along which a young red-headed boy was hurriedly making his way. His progress brought him to the end of the walkway and up the stairs to the tier of seats immediately in front of the old man and the girls. There he took a seat between a man and woman right in front of them. The pensive look on the boy's face alerted those near him that a revelation of his activities might be forthcoming.

Looking again at the walkway, the Elder Statesman spied a campus policeman slowly walking on the young boy's trail. In a few minutes, he arrived at the place where the red-headed lad was cowering.

"Does he belong to you?" the officer asked the man and woman between whom the boy was sitting.

"Yes, he does. What has he done now?" the woman wanted to know.

"He has been down there throwing cups of water on the fans below him," said the unsmiling officer. "Either you keep him with you, or you can pick him up outside the stadium after the game," he informed her.

Weighing the evidence against him and pondering what the after-game consequences of his escapades might be, that red-headed boy was much subdued and became a model citizen for the duration of the contest.

Retribution. How swift!

Riding the Wave

The allure of the shrimping season captured the imagination of Bert, Ivan, and Wesley.

"I have a shrimp net and a boat," said Bert. "We can go down to Balfour County and launch the boat, and in a few hours, we will have all the shrimp the three of us want."

The other two purred in agreement.

The following Saturday, Bert picked up Ivan and Wesley before daylight. A-shrimping they would go. Upon arriving at the launching ramp at a quarter after eight, they quickly launched the boat and headed out into deeper water. Soon they lowered the net to make their first drag. They brought in some shrimp but not as many as they expected. They kept making drags and moving farther out as the morning hours crept by. Other boats out in the bay were passing them with occupants waving.

"People out here on the bay sure are friendly," said Wesley.

"Yeah they are," agreed Ivan.

In a few minutes, Bert noticed that they were the only ones still out in the bay. Looking to the southwest, he saw a line of low, dark clouds rapidly approaching. "I think maybe those friendly people were not waving but were pointing at that approaching squall line. We had better haul this net in and get out of here," he said with alarm in his voice. Bert had served four years in the navy and seen many squall lines. He knew what they could do, especially to a small boat.

Just as they got the net secured, the first wave crashed into them. Although a lot of water came into the boat, it did not sink. Neither did the water go over the motor. Bert started the motor and maneuvered the boat up onto the front of the next wave.

"I don't know where this wave is going, but we are going to ride it to shore," he said.

Bert ran the motor and guided the boat while Wesley grabbed a bucket and bailed water like a man possessed. Ivan was panic-stricken and remained motionless for several minutes. Finally, he grabbed all three life preservers, put one on in the normal fashion, and then strapped one around each of his legs. Lastly, he lay down flat in the bottom of the boat and held on to the gunnels with both hands.

The wave carried the boat to the Balfour County shore, not far from the launching ramp. The squall line quickly passed, but that three-man crew had had enough. Bert backed the boat out from shore and then guided it down to the boat ramp, where they quickly loaded it onto the trailer.

When they came to a restaurant near Bay St. Mark, they stopped to get some coffee in hopes it would drive the chill from their bones.

While seated in a booth, drinking coffee, Ivan exclaimed, "I hope you two realize that I saved your lives back there on the bay!"

"What do you mean you saved our lives?" shouted Bert.

"Yeah," chimed Wesley. "All you did was lay flat down in the bottom of the boat."

"Yes, but I kept the boat balanced so it would not capsize," protested Ivan.

Had Wesley not restrained him, Bert would have choked Ivan to his knees.

Roll Down the Window

The business acumen of the Elder Statesman was legendary in the village of Rough Edge. Timber, farms, cattle, and rental properties were all included in his holdings. The conduct of such varied business interests necessitated a lot of travel. Usually, he got his nephew, Chester, to drive him wherever he wanted to go.

He had seven rental houses in Mobile. He arranged for Chester to drive him to Mobile on Friday mornings to collect the rents.

"Be here at six o'clock," said the Elder Statesman with a note of urgency in his voice. "I want to get back home before noon."

Dawn that Friday broke clear, bright, and freezing cold. Thick frost gave a white tinge to the outdoors. Anticipating a comfortable ride in the pickup with the heater discharging volumes of warm air, Chester dressed as usual in a light jacket. He was in the frigid outside air just long enough to go from the house to the truck.

Sometimes the Elder Statesman chewed tobacco, and that Friday happened to be one of those days. When he came out of the house, Chester could see the bulge in his jaw where the chew of tobacco was nestled comfortably. The Elder Statesman wore one of those World War I army trench coats. It was about half an inch thick and made of wool. It reached from his chin to his knees and was buttoned all the way down.

When he got in the truck, the first thing the man in the wool cocoon did was roll the window all the way down so he could discharge the tobacco juice. As they traveled down Highway 45 at fifty miles an hour, the wind gushed in through the open window, circled around the Elder Statesman, and went straight down Chester's collar. Chester was in total shivering misery. Halfway to Mobile, the old man noticed Charlie's fingers had turned blue and that he was shaking uncontrollably. "Is that too much air for you, Chester?" he asked.

"Yes, sir," Chester mumbled through chattering teeth.

"Well, roll your window down and let some of it out!" crowed the old man.

Sheriff Deadeye
and Spiked Tea

The consanguinity of the Elder Statesman and Sheriff Deadeye resulted in the two of them being connoisseurs of the culinary delights offered by the many watering holes in Mobile that they patronized. Buffet-style restaurants, steak houses, seafood establishments, and barbecue specialties—they frequented them all. Sheriff Deadeye—a sobriquet the oldest daughter of the Elder Statesman had earned for being a superb rifle shot—was always eager to try out new eateries all over the city and out on the Mobile Bay causeway. They had feasted on a flounder so large that it overlapped the platter on which it was served at an establishment on the Dauphin Island Parkway. Salad and roast prime rib so tender that it fell apart at the slightest touch of a fork had invigorated their taste buds.

The Elder Statesman had an appointment in Mobile on one of those hot, humid summer dog days—a day perfectly suited for enjoying spicy barbecued beef ribs. The merest hint of a trip to Mobile engaged Sheriff Deadeye's mental review of the barbecue places in Mobile, from which she selected M.B.'s out on Airport Boulevard. The day arrived, and they departed from Rough Edge at 9:00 a.m. The appointment was over at noon. Thirty minutes later, the enticing aroma of barbecued beef assaulted their olfactory organs as they entered M.B.'s, where they took a seat in a booth. The wait was only a few minutes, but wave after wave of mouthwatering scents made it seem like hours to the ravenously hungry duo.

Momentarily, a courteous young waitress inquired what refreshment the two anxiously waiting people wanted with their dinner.

"Sweet tea," they both chimed at the same time.

The tea arrived at the table a few minutes later, but it was not sweet enough for the Elder Statesman. The old man looked for the sugar and spied a glass on the table with a spout for discharging its white granular contents. Supposing this to be sugar, he poured a spoonful into his tea. Sheriff Deadeye's expression of disbelief hinted that something was amiss. It turned out that the sugar was in packets behind the napkin holder, out of the Elder Statesman's sight. He had put salt in his tea. Sheriff Deadeye laughed so hard that tears ran down her cheeks, especially when the old man drank the spiked tea rather than tell the waitress what he had done and ask for new glass. She still cracks up every time the salted tea is mentioned.

Snakes and Popsicles

Willie Prince held his nervous tension in abeyance until exterior stimuli stirred a reaction within him. The prompt response was usually reflexive in nature and not a calculated, well-reasoned action.

Willie and his wife, Mary, journeyed forth to Jackson for the sole purpose of trading their old vehicle in for a new pickup. Once their business successfully concluded, they headed for home. Nothing dramatic marred the trip until about halfway between Jefferson and Carson. Willie spied a huge rattlesnake crossing the highway. As his new truck headed toward the snake, his nervous tension burst forth into a dominating intention to run the creature over and kill it. Forthwith, he felt the bump when the wheels ran over the snake.

Looking in the rearview mirror, Willie could not see the injured serpent, whereupon he concluded, "Mary, that snake must be hung under the truck. What to do in this situation," he wondered aloud.

Willie, being totally fearful of snakes, was not about to get out of the truck until he knew its whereabouts. Turning the truck crosswise on the highway, Willie began bouncing off the road and across the ditch, attempting to dislodge the snake. He backed up and repeated the procedure numerous times, asking his wife after each repetition, "Do you see it, Mary?"

He was still jumping the ditch when Mack drove up. "What in the world are you doing, Willie?" Mack asked.

Willie explained in such an excited jumble of words that it took a few minutes for Mack to understand the gist of what had happened.

"I hate to tell you, Willie, but you killed the snake. It is on the side of the road about a hundred yards back toward Jefferson," Mack informed him.

The Elder Statesman happened to be in the automotive dealership, having his car's oil changed, when Willie came in to have his truck checked. After some time, the shop foreman came in to talk to Willie.

"I'm afraid your truck is totaled. All that jumping the ditch warped the frame," he said.

"We just bought this truck. Mary and I never even made it home with it," Willie lamented.

Some weeks later, Willie entered the break room to get a drink and a snack. Wilbur, standing at the microwave with a popsicle, had one of those inspired moments. He placed the popsicle in the microwave and waited for Willie to approach. When he got close, Wilbur opened the microwave, took the popsicle out, and bit a huge chunk out of it.

"Oh boy, is that good!" he said, licking his lips. "Willie, you don't know what good is until you cook a popsicle in a microwave," Wilbur said as he nonchalantly walked away.

A few days later, Willie got a popsicle out of a vending machine, put it in the microwave, set it on thirty seconds, and hit start. When he opened the door, melted goo was all over the inside of the microwave. Wilbur had set him up again!

Static

I t was positively ingenious the way H.V. proved that he was not an electrical engineer. Like most college students, he carried with him several items that really were not necessary in the furtherance of his education. H.V. and his roommate, the Elder Statesman, resided in Hardy Hall, room 212-C. Between them, they had three radios.

When time permitted, H.V. would turn on one of the radios and tune in to a station playing good music. Soon he discovered that music accompanied by static was most unpleasant to hear. Surely, he reasoned, there must be a way to get better reception.

"Perhaps, you need a better antenna for the radio," suggested the Elder Statesman.

"You're right," concurred H.V., whereupon he set about creating one.

After breaking out his tool kit, he extracted the antenna from one of the other radios. The antenna was just a coil of wire wound around a wooden core about a half inch in diameter and six inches long. Within a few minutes, H.V. had the extracted antenna connected to the antenna of the radio he was playing. He now had music with improved static. The reception was better but not as good as he wanted. H.V. took the third radio, removed its antenna, and connected it up so that he had three antennas hooked to one radio. Better still, but H.V. wanted perfection. Wondering what else he could do, he spied the window screen.

"I know," he said excitedly to the Elder Statesman. "I'll hook this radio with the three antennas to the window screen, and I'll get better reception."

Soon he had the radio hooked up to the window screen. The static dropped to a near tolerable level, but H.V. was still not satisfied. At length, he caught sight of the water pipes under the sink.

He yelled with glee, "I'll make the whole dormitory my antenna."

He grabbed the radio, snatched it loose from the window screen, carried it over to the sink, and sat down in a chair. He took the antenna wire and reached under the sink to attach it to the water pipe, but he forgot one very important thing: the water pipe formed a direct electrical ground. When the antenna wire got about an inch from the water pipe, there was an electrical arc as bright as a flash of lightning. The Elder Statesman had not seen such an atmospheric disturbance since Hurricane Camille hit the Gulf Coast.

H.V. fell back onto the bed, violently trying to shake the electrical shock from his hand. Success. H.V. had conclusively proven that he was not an electrical engineer. He had also gotten rid of some of the stuff not needed in the furtherance of his education. Namely, three radios.

Teller of Tales

In the days of yore when the Elder Statesman was a young man, a chapping, cold winter wind impelled him and a few friends to loose the dogs and rush into the woods to go coon hunting. Catching a coon was of secondary importance. Weaving elasticity into the veracity of the stories related by hunters as they warmed themselves by a fire while waiting for the dogs to tree superseded all other motivational influences for enduring a night out in the freezing cold.

There was no call to order a meeting of the gathered hunters. No teller of tales was recognized by a duly elected moderator. There was not a published agenda listing the subjects up for discussion. Subjects ranged from politics, to hunting, to disasters, to football, to the macabre, and to a hundred other things. The entire proceedings were characterized by spontaneity.

One of the sagacious members of the panel of hunters put forth the notion that mankind had built great dams and bridges, had mastered the techniques of flying, and had even sent men to the moon. In light of these accomplishments, he concluded that nothing was impossible for man. Daniel, the Elder Statesman's brother-in-law, entered the proposition that there was one thing that man could not do.

"And just what is that?" queried Leroy.

"You can't straddle a mud puddle with a wheelbarrow," replied Daniel.

After scratchings of heads and a round of murmuring, all the hunters nodded in agreement. The conversation, like the fire, died down considerably, allowing a pause for the group to listen for the dogs. The distinctive quality of the hounds barking let the hunters know that they were still trailing.

"That must be a big coon for it to take so long for the dogs to tree it," opined Leroy while throwing more wood on the glowing coals.

The heat of the fire once again elicited verbal absurdities from the men. Added to that was the vocal liberation achieved by imbibing the strong flavor of spirits contained in a little brown jug that had been brought along to warm the hunters' interiors. Rational thought of an individual hunter was reduced in proportion to the depth of his imbibing.

Thus, with a total absence of lucidity, Daniel remembered a friend and asked, "Is Billy Jack still dead?"

With even less lucidity, Leroy replied, "I hope so 'cause we buried him last September."

Ten Degrees of Cool

Big Boy, as he was affectionately known by his fellow traffic foremen, came by that name honestly. He was a former college football player weighing in at 289 pounds. His job as the receiving foreman required him to cover the whole yard. He spent most days walking from one area to another, checking on his different crews and spotting trucks coming into the plant in the proper place to be unloaded. Big Boy sweated much in the summertime, so he carried a large red bandanna in his pocket and regularly used it to wipe the beads of moisture from his face.

The Elder Statesman's office was one of several that Big Boy stopped at to cool off for a minute or two.

"Big Boy, why don't you stop this constant running up and down the streets? Your men will page you on your radio when they need you. You get red-faced, hot, and sweaty with your shirttail hanging out, wiping with that red bandanna, and then come in my office and soak up ten degrees of cool," the old man said to him.

"I can't. I've too much to see about," complained Big Boy.

"When the supervisors come out and see me sitting at my desk with my feet propped up and trucks being loaded, they know I have everything under control. They see you running up and down the street all hot and bothered and they think you are fighting a battle. That is why I get a good raise every year and you wind up complaining about yours," the Elder Statesman retorted to Big Boy, just as he had done many times before.

The Elder Statesman planned to retire three months later on January 10. The last week of December, the company passed out to the salaried personnel their annual raises. The old man decided to teach Big Boy a lesson before he left to devote himself full-time to his fish business. He typed out a duplicate of the paper showing his raise, only he changed the amount to a much larger figure.

When Big Boy came into the office, the Elder Statesman handed him the duplicate and said nonchalantly, "In two weeks, I will be retired, so I don't care if you know what my raise would have been next year. Take a look at it and you will see what I've been telling you."

Big Boy took the paper and read it. The transformation was dramatic and immediate. A pale Big Boy's lips began to tremble. With shaking hand, he reached back for the doorknob, turned it, and stumbled out backward without uttering a word. With a dazed expression on his pale face, and still gripping the paper, Big Boy began to stagger down the street.

"You had better go get him and straighten that out. He is going to have a heart attack if you don't," Terry advised the Elder Statesman.

The old man ran out and caught Big Boy, turned him around, and brought him back into the office, where he showed him the real paper.

The next day, Big Boy came into the office pallid and stressed out. He announced, "I didn't sleep a wink all night. I just couldn't get that raise business off my mind, but I'll make it up this summer when I soak up ten degrees of cool every day."

The Biggest Liar in Whitney County

The usual gathering of old men was seated on the bench in front of the post office. They had about exhausted the random topics of conversation. The weather, the best place to hunt on the opening day of deer season, and what crops had been harvested had all been addressed by the Elder Statesman, L.J., Rudy, and Woodrow in infinite detail by the time Moody drove up in his pickup. In the northeast quadrant of Whitney County, Moody was known as a world-class liar.

Upon exiting his truck, Moody walked over to the group seated on the bench to join in the conversation.

Forthwith, he said, "Rudy, you know where that gopher hole is out in the piney woods by the big poplar? It is right next to the road, you know. I was driving by there last week when I saw what I thought as a large tree limb lying across the road. I stopped to move it, but lo, it turned out to be a huge rattlesnake. It was headed for that gopher hole to den up for the winter. Luckily, I had John's shotgun with me and I killed him with it. That snake was so big, if its head were held up to the eaves of the post office, its tail would reach the ground."

All of the old men on the bench gave a skeptical nod. After ending his story, Moody got his mail and left the amused men seated on the bench.

The Elder Statesman observed, "Mighty big snake. It's over nine feet from the ground to the eaves of the post office. We all know he was lying, but just one time I would like to catch him at it."

Rudy chimed in, "We've caught him this time. You know that shotgun of John's that he said he killed that snake with? Well, it is standing in the corner of my bedroom and has a spider web in the end of the barrel."

While the old men laughed at Moody's snake story, he was on his way to Jackson to get a haircut. He entered Caldwell's Barbershop and took a seat in one of the barber chairs. Being a very glib gentleman, Moody began chatting with the barber.

"The other day, I was out in the piney woods when I caught sight of a drove of turkeys approaching. I hid behind some gallberry bushes and waited. Before long, they came within range of my shotgun. I took careful aim and shot into a group of the birds and had the good luck to kill four turkeys with that one shot."

The man getting his hair cut in the next chair turned to Moody and said, "You didn't know that I am a state game warden, did you?"

Without skipping a beat, Moody replied, "No, and you didn't know that you are talking to the biggest liar in Whitney County, did you?"

The Case of the Bug-Eyed Bible Salesman

Moe L. was an avid deer hunter. The woods around Rough Edge were well-stocked with deer, which gave him plenty of opportunity to practice that particular art form. In that practice, he spent every spare minute in the woods.

It so happened that Ole E.D. planned to go hunting with Moe L. on Saturday. He stopped by Moe L.'s house to finalize their plans. Janice, Moe L.'s wife, was sweeping the front porch when he arrived. After informing him that Moe L. was working evenings, she began relating to Ole E.D. what Moe L. had told her about Saturday's hunting plans.

While they were talking, the Elder Statesman drove up. He was included in the plans for Saturday. After several minutes of talking, Janice offered to make them a cup of coffee. Since they often came by Moe L.'s and drank coffee, they readily accepted her offer.

"Come on inside and have a seat while I fix the coffee," she said. The aroma of coffee soon filled the kitchen and living room.

The sound of a vehicle outside was soon followed by a knock on the door. When Janice opened it, a young man introduced himself and informed her that he was a college student selling Bibles to help pay for his college expenses. He was promptly invited in and directed to a chair. While Janice returned to the kitchen to pour the coffee, the young man turned to the Elder Statesman and asked, "Are you Mr. Faith?"

"No, I am not," responded the Elder Statesman.

Turning to Ole E.D., the young man repeated the question, to which Ole E.D. replied, "I am a Mr. Faith, but I don't live here."

The young man's eyes widened and his eyebrows shot up as he wondered what kind of situation he had walked into. To say that two men in the house with another man's wife made that Bible salesman nervous would be a great understatement. He was barely able to present his sales pitch to Janice.

It so happened that a breakdown had occurred in the part of the paper mill where Moe L. worked, and he'd been sent home for the day. Moe L. saw the time off as a great opportunity to go hunting if he rushed home, grabbed his gun, and headed for the woods. Forthwith, his pickup roared into the yard. He dashed across the yard and up the steps, jerked the door open, hurried across the living room without looking at or speaking to anyone, and entered his bedroom, where he kept his shotgun in the closet. Momentarily, there was no mistaking the sound of shells entering the gun as Moe L. loaded it.

All of the color drained from the Bible salesman's face, and his trembling hands revealed the panic that had seized him. When Moe L. reentered the living room carrying his now-loaded shotgun, that Bible salesman just knew he was about to be caught up in the middle of a killing.

The Elder Statesman thought he would have to tackle that college student to keep him from breaking out of the door, leaving all his sample Bibles behind. Janice finally resolved the situation by explaining that Moe L. (her husband), Ole E.D., and the Elder Statesman were cousins.

Whether or not it was of any consequence to the bug-eyed Bible salesman, I do not know, but Janice purchased a large family Bible from him. He did not linger after the sale.

The Catfish Man

The Elder Statesman was an enterprising man. Of the several business ventures he had established, none was conducted with more vigor than his catfish project. Over a period of years, he built seventeen ponds and stocked them with fish. The project grew to such a size that he began buying fish feed by the truckload. He even built a fish hatchery so he could raise his own fingerlings.

His farm happened to be adjacent to a large creek. Inevitably, creatures inhabiting the creek bottom found their way to the Elder Statesman's ponds. Otters, snakes, and turtles all took up residence in his ponds, where they consumed his fingerlings. He battled them constantly. Each time he drained a pond to harvest the fish, he carried a rifle with which to shoot the invaders.

Once when draining a pond, he encountered a gator about two feet long. In a moment of inspiration, he decided not to shoot it but rather to capture it alive and have a little fun with it. After a few attempts, the Elder Statesman managed to scoop it up with a large dip net. The gator was soon securely tied with a heavy nylon cord. The catfish man was now ready for a new adventure.

Quite a few establishments in Rough Edge provided stronger flavors of the spirits available for their patrons. The Elder Statesman certainly enjoyed sampling many of those flavors. As was the custom, all those watering holes were dimly lit affairs. A man could relax, slowly consume his drinks, and engage in idle conversation with his friends without attracting any attention. Into the White Castle Bar strode the catfish man with his gator in tow. He took a seat at a table with a couple of his friends and tied the gator to it. Naturally, he had to tell his friends all about capturing the gator.

"Other folks have their guard doges, but I've got a guard gator," he gushed between sips. "I'll just keep him tied in the yard and nobody will ever come messing around my house," he mused.

The Elder Statesman did not notice the time slipping by. All the while, the cumulative effect of the drinks manifested itself in the slight slurring of his speech and the less well-coordinated movement of his hand as he raised his glass for another sip. Under the influence of the volume consumed, the Elder Statesman roused himself from his seat, untied his gator, unsteadily walked to the bar, and took a seat on a bar stool with the intention of showing his gator to the bartender.

When he plopped the gator down on the bar, the patrons next to him shouted, "Get that thing away from me."

Needless to say, the bartender was not amused. Motioning to a bouncer, the bartender had the catfish man escorted from that dimly lit den.

There was nothing left for the Elder Statesman to do except get into his pickup truck and weave his way home. It was nearly midnight when he turned into his driveway. In his bleary-eyed condition, he was unable to insert his key into the door lock. He banged on the door until his very sleepy wife got up and let him in.

He blubbered to her, "They threw me and my gator out of the White Castle Bar tonight." She was even less amused than the bartender. Pushing his luck to the ultimate limit, he demanded of his wife, "Where is my supper?"

She growled back at him, "It was on the table at six o'clock. You were not here, so I fixed you a plate and put it in the oven."

She turned and went back to bed in a huff without telling him that the light in the oven had burned out and that she had removed it and put it into her purse to take to town the next day so she could get another one like it.

The Elder Statesman wobbled over to the stove, opened the oven door, and reached in to retrieve his supper. Unsteady as he reached in, he stuck his finger into the light socket and got the shock of his life. His scream disturbed the peace of the entire household.

Upon relating this adventure to me, he complained, "The worst thing about the whole affair was that the shock sobered me up."

The Celebration

The Elder Statesman and his friends at MSU used any pretext to go out and celebrate. The night of the first Ali versus Liston fight arrived, generating speculation as to who the winner would be. Some thought the super-strong mauler Liston was sure to win, but others believed Ali, who moved as gracefully as a ballerina, would be victorious. The debaters decided to listen to the match on the radio.

Willie, Big John, Tom, Henry, and the Elder Statesman piled into Willie's 1956 Oldsmobile. Thirty minutes later, they were sitting in the parking lot of the Red Wolf Club, a beer joint in Calhoun, Mississippi, sipping on ice-cold beer and listening to the preliminaries of the boxing match.

Henry said as he got out of the car, "I'm going to get another beer before the fight."

Several minutes later, he returned with his beer and was greeted with Willie's announcement: "Well, you missed it. Ali knocked Liston out."

A much-dejected Henry stated, "Let's go get a bite to eat while we are in Calhoun."

The tribe of boxing fans went to a hole-in-the-wall pizza parlor down near MSCW and ordered a deep-dish pizza. Steam rose from a pizza so hot that the cheese on top bubbled as the waitress placed it on the table. The five men looking over the pizza created a reasonable facsimile of hungry vultures perched on tree limbs above the dead body of some forest creature.

The aroma of the pizza overcame Henry. He took a spoon and dipped into the bubbling mass, retrieving a glob of the steaming mixture, which he raised to his mouth. Henry's eyes narrowed to mere slits to avoid the steam issuing forth from his spoonful of pizza. Barely able to see, Henry tried to blow on the steaming mass to cool it but by mistake touched it to his lips. The boiling, steaming cheese stuck to his lips, making his eyes and mouth pop open wide in painful panic.

Not saying a word, he stretched both hands above the table, spreading all his fingers wide apart, while his wide-open and watering eyes scanned the table for something with which to cool his blistered lips. Spying a glass of water, he snatched it up, placed the rim under his lower lip, and tilted the glass upward. A smile of relief spread across his face as the icy water cooled the sizzling cheese clinging to his lips. Just as the passengers that survived the sinking of the *Titanic* never forgot that experience, Henry would never forget his experiences the night that Ali defeated Liston to win the heavyweight boxing crown.

Henry fatigued himself explaining to all the questioning students he met how he got those lovely blisters protruding from his lips. Such are the problems students sometimes encounter when they go out celebrating.

The Cell Bull

The Elder Statesman, being well-versed in history, understood the corruption that led to the Protestant Reformation in the late Middle Ages. Martin Luther consolidated those corruptions into the *Ninety-Five Theses*, which in 1715 he nailed to the door of the church in Wittenberg, Germany. From the Reformation set in motion by Luther's theses, the Elder Statesman realized that reformative steps could be taken by individuals, especially when external motivational pressure was applied to their lives.

The old man was contemplating such a view when Martin came into his office. Martin was an African-American forklift operator in the Elder Statesman's crew at the plant where they worked. He also happened to be the pastor of a local church.

"How did it happen that you became a preacher?" the old man asked Martin.

"Well, you see," replied Martin, "I have a sister that lives in the Happy Hills area of Mobile. One weekend, I went down there to visit her and her family. I went out on the town Saturday night. Like so many foolish young men, I overdid the beer drinking, winding up stoned out of my mind. My sister lived in one end of a duplex. When I got back to the duplex, I went to the wrong end and tried to get inside. The occupants of that apartment thought I was trying to break in to rob them, so they called the police. When the police arrived, the occupants of that apartment came out and told their story. I was arrested and, despite my protests, was dragged off the porch. I began to resist the officers. Grabbing a short piece of two-by-four that was lying on the porch, I took a swing at one of the policemen. That officer snatched a spring-loaded billy club off his belt and rapped me between the eyes three times before I hit the floor out cold.

"I came to in the holding cell of the Mobile City jail. About twenty men were in that cell, including one huge muscular man called The Cell Bull. When a meal was served, The Cell Bull took whatever he wanted off anyone's plate, and he took all the sample packs of cigarettes."

"What did you give him, Martin?" asked the Elder Statesman.

"Whatever he wanted," said Martin, his eyes widening in terror at the thought of The Cell Bull.

"One man refused to give The Cell Bull his cigarettes. The Cell Bull grabbed that man by the neck and the seat of his pants, walked over to the bars of the cell, and jammed his head through them. They had to get a man with a cutting torch to remove one of the bars to free that man. Then and there I vowed to walk the straight and narrow when I got out of jail. I guess you could say the cop with the billy club beat the hell out of me and The Cell Bull led me to repentance. There was nothing left for me to do except go to preaching."

The Cold-Water Treatment

The early years of marriage, the years of the most adjusting, have unlimited potential for long remembered adventures. The Elder Statesman's marriage to Lillian exceeded the norm in that category.

To the Elder Statesman, Saturday was the one day he had to take care of any project requiring several hours of labor. He often needed Lillian to hand him tools or to hold some item while he worked on it. He liked for her to get up and get ready for the day by eight o'clock, while she interpreted Saturday morning as the time God gave her to sleep late. A point of adjustment definitely loomed on the horizon.

After a long stretch of calling Lillian to get up early one Saturday morning, the Elder Statesman heard her drowsily reply, "Come back and wake me up in thirty minutes."

The Elder Statesman decided that drastic action was needed to end this most annoying habit. One Friday night before going to bed, he put a glass about one-third full of water into the refrigerator. The next morning, he—the sly schemer—went to the refrigerator, retrieved his glass of cold water, went to the bedroom, and called Lillian.

She sang the same old tune: "Come back and wake me up in half an hour."

This time, the Elder Statesman threw the covers back and dashed the cold water in her face while saying, "No! It's time to get up."

She sprang to her feet so quickly, it looked as if she were spring-loaded. The things she said and the names she called him cannot be found even in a sailor's lexicon. It took a few days for the fuming to end, but finally things got back to normal.

Quite a few years went by without another thought about the cold-water treatment. But Lillian had a long memory. Late one afternoon, the Elder Statesman was taking a shower. Lillian had prepared for and anxiously awaited this moment. Several days earlier, she had put a full glass of water in the refrigerator for just this opportunity. She got the glass of cold water and poured half of it into another glass. Slipping quietly into the bathroom, she tossed the contents of the first glass over the shower curtain. She laughed with glee when she heard the Elder Statesman gasp for breath as the cold water cascaded down his bare back.

After a minute or two, he was sufficiently recovered to continue his shower. That was when the second glass of cold water hit him. Lillian was completely satisfied that this point of adjustment in their marriage was now complete. She went back to the kitchen, humming a snappy little tune.

The Courtesies
of Football

F
ond memories of long-ago football seasons in which
he played a lineman for the Leroy Bruins caroused
around in the cranial cavity of the Elder Statesman.
In his older years, failing eyesight rendered him incapable of
driving at night. Calling his friend, Ole E.D., he proposed
that if E.D. would drive them to the local games, he would
pay for their tickets. The proposal was accepted in time for
the season opener.

The two left Rough Edge with plenty of time to get
a good parking place close to the stadium. The Elder
Statesman bought their tickets, and upon entering the south
gate, they made their way to the fifty-yard line, where they
selected seats a little over halfway up in the stands. Soon the
stands filled up. The band played the national anthem. A
local minister offered up an invocation. The team captains
met with the officials in the center of the field to select
which goal to defend and which team would receive the
opening kickoff. A whistle blew, and the game began.

Courtesy, a highly desirable trait, is totally devoid in many of the more rabid football fans. Four men from Leroy went to every game and always sat together near the fifty-yard line a few tiers below the center of the stands. They were a little to the left and two tiers below Ole E.D. and the Elder Statesman. Every time the opposing team got the ball, the four men would stand up and continuously yell, "Defense, defense," while punching up into the air with clenched fists. The cheering activity of the four men blocked the view of those behind them.

The old man groused, "They should have charged us half price. We can only see half of the game."

After several repetitions of the standing performance, the Elder Statesman decided to convince at least one of the four that their conduct was disturbing and unacceptable. He unwrapped a stick of chewing gum and inserted it into his mouth. Working his mandible rapidly, he soon converted the gum into a sticky wad. The next time the quartet stood to perform, the old man took the gum and gave it an underhanded lob. It landed on the seat under one of the cheering men.

"If he will not remain seated, I will stick him to the bleacher by the seat of his pants," the Elder Statesman said with a devious smile.

Later that season, the Elder Statesman and E.D. journeyed to Churchwell to see the rivals battle it out under cloudy skies. It was a close, exciting game, which they enjoyed until it began to rain. Fortunately, the Elder Statesman had brought his umbrella with him. He opened it and held it so they both were sheltered from the rain.

Tim was seated directly in front of the old man. His torso had expanded to the point that the buttons of his shirt stretched the cloth surrounding his midsection. The stretching action pulled the shirttail out of his pants, revealing the part of his anatomy where the cleavage of his buttocks began.

"Watch this. I am going to have a little fun with Tim," the old man said in a low tone.

He tilted the umbrella so that most of the rain ran off the front edge. Then he skillfully maneuvered it until a small stream of water struck Tim exactly where the cleavage began and followed the natural channel to regions below. Tim never realized that he was getting more than the natural rainfall.

The Day the Elder Statesman Cried

Jeff, the Elder Statesman's uncle, was blessed to have four sons, two of whom served four years in the navy aboard aircraft carriers. After their years of service, the two sons returned home, went to work—one at a chemical plant and the other at a paper mill—and raised families. Jeff, unfortunately, was an alcoholic, and the abuse of that substance led to his premature demise. Elton, the oldest son, followed in his father's footsteps.

As the years passed, Elton's life went into a downward spiral. He first lost his job. After that, he worked for the county and later as a security guard at a local plant, but he never made the money he was used to. The reduced funds put a lot of stress on his family. To make more money, Elton went to work with a seismic crew and moved to Texas. Good times for the family were not to be.

While in Texas working with the seismic crew on a large ranch, he became severely ill. Doctors at the hospital he was sent to could not determine whether he had some kind of virus or had come into contact with a dangerous chemical.

X-rays showed that his lungs had some sort of coating in them. To save his life, the doctors gave him massive doses of cortisone. Those doses would have a detrimental effect on Elton a few years later.

When Elton returned home from Texas with no job, his brother let him and his family live in a house he owned that was old but usable. Stress piled up to the point that Elton's wife left him. Then the effect of the cortisone began to manifest itself in the form of deteriorating hip joints. Soon he had to have both hip joints replaced. He was put in a full-body cast while the joints healed. He was in that body cast when Hurricane Fredrick came through. His brothers had to take care of him during that storm because Elton was helpless.

The Elder Statesman reached out to him after he got out of the cast, and for a while, Elton lived well enough. The Elder Statesman gave him a Bible and wrote a message inside it to Elton. But the good time was not to last. Elton lifted the bottle again, and this time he could not put it down. A few months later, he was in a motel room on the Mississippi Gulf Coast. The years of alcohol abuse caught up with him. He began to hemorrhage and, unable to get help, bled to death. More than a hundred empty beer cans were scattered over the motel room floor when they found him.

The police found the name of the Elder Statesman in the Bible he had given Elton and called him. After explaining what they had found, they asked if the Elder Statesman would notify some of Elton's family so that they could come and identify his body. Elton's youngest brother was working for the county at that time. The county crew was busy working right in front of the Elder Statesman's house. With a heavy heart, the Elder Statesman told the youngest brother that Elton was dead. The younger brother left work and went home.

The next youngest brother came out of the woods across the road on his tractor. The old man flagged him down and broke the news to him also. When he called the last brother's wife at work, she told him that brother was off working on his farm. The Elder Statesman rode out to the farm and relayed the same information to him.

It was a terrible day for the Elder Statesman, having to bear the news of Elton's death to his three brothers, who were also the old man's cousins. That day, the Elder Statesman cried.

The Double Dipper

Though not a troglodyte, Joe had mastered the art of being gauche to the nth degree. When one of his absurdities burst forth in exquisitely undeniable clarity, Joe would confront his observers with a blank, uncomprehending stare. The Elder Statesman had traversed this territory many times before when he hired Joe to do odd jobs around his place.

The Elder Statesman created seventeen flower beds for his wife so he would not have to mow around individual flowers stuck all over the yard. Nine of those beds were created by pouring cement walks around the house. The old man hired Joe to help him pour those sidewalks. Each morning they made three pours forty-five inches wide, four inches thick, and ten feet long until the project was complete. Joe mixed the cement by hand while the old man spread the pour, put a smooth finish on it, and edged the cement before it became too stiff to work.

Every time Joe started to mix another batch, he asked the Elder Statesman how much sand, cement, and gravel to use.

"One shovel of cement, two shovels of sand, and three shovels of gravel," the exasperated old man repeated twenty times a day.

After each repetition, that blank stare engulfed Joe's entire countenance as he mumbled, "Oh."

On the final day of the project, they only worked one hour. The next day, they went to Mobile to take a tiller to a shop for an engine repair. They dropped the tiller off and, as it was near noon, went to Madison's to eat dinner.

The Elder Statesman stated to Joe, "I will buy your dinner today in lieu of writing a ten-dollar check for that last hour of work you did on the sidewalks."

Joe replied, "I'm OK with that."

Passing down the cafeteria line in the restaurant, the Elder Statesman was astounded as he watched Joe get red beans and rice, half a fried chicken, three side dishes, peach pie, a salad, cornbread, and iced tea.

The old man thought, *If he eats all that, I'll have to carry him out of here.*

Not only did he eat the two entrees, the sides, the dessert, the salad, and the bread, but he didn't burp a single time. Joe's entire extravaganza cost the old man twenty-three dollars. When the Elder Statesman confronted him with the fact that he had gotten two entrees and that his dinner had cost more than twice as much as he was due to be paid, the uncomprehending stare took up residence on Joe's face once again!

"I learned a lesson today," the vexed old man said. "From now on, I am going to call you D.D. Harris, the D.D. standing for double dipper."

The EASE of the Hunt

Deer hunters are a rare, adventurous breed. Sometimes their endeavors to get a buck in their sights are ingenious, but some are ridiculously insane. The Elder Statesman was renowned for employing both methods.

Green patches will attract deer, so the Elder Statesman always planted three or four scattered about on his place. By the time the season would open, the green stuff would have sprouted and deer would be keeping it trimmed to about two inches high. The old man did not see any logical reason to perch on a tree limb in total discomfort. Neither did he want to risk a fall from a ladder stand or pay the expense of building a shooting house. He opted for comfort without the risk of falling and without the cost.

He had at home a well-worn discarded recliner. Loading it on his pickup, the Elder Statesman took it to his favorite green patch. He hooked a block and tackle to a limb up in a large oak tree, secured one end of the cable to the chair, and attached the other end to the bumper of his pickup.

After pulling it up the tree, he placed the recliner on one of the large limbs and secured the back to the trunk. Next, he tied two ropes to a limb within easy reach of the recliner and dropped the loose ends to the ground. All this was done several days in advance of his first hunt.

The Saturday afternoon of the first hunt in total comfort finally arrived. The old man carried ammo in his jacket's cargo pockets, a .270 rifle with a strap over his shoulder, and a case of beer under his arm. Upon arriving at the prepared tree stand, he tied one of the drop lines to the .270 and the other one around the case of beer. Momentarily, he climbed up the cleats he had previously nailed up the tree trunk, sank down in the recliner, and pulled up the ropes—first the beer and then his rifle.

Now this is the way to hunt, the Elder Statesman thought as he popped open his first can of beer. Soon he had drained that first can, so he dropped it down through the tree limbs. The can sounded like musical chimes as it clinked its way down, bouncing from limb to limb. Draining several more cans and dropping them in similar fashion continued the clinking uproar.

The Elder Statesman told his buddies at work, "Only one little yearling came into the patch, and it was nervous."

One morning, the Elder Statesman and three friends were hunting deer with dogs. It often happened that a deer got by the standers, which was exactly what occurred that morning. The old man picked up one of the standers in his truck and informed him that they were going around by the highway to cut the dogs off. Speed was of the essence.

At a place where the road curved, a dirt road entered the highway. An inebriated individual was sitting in a pickup in the dirt road. As they came around that curve in the speeding pickup, the old man and his friend met a state forestry truck that was hauling a bulldozer. Just as they met, the inebriated man pulled out into the highway, knocking the Elder Statesman's pickup into the tandem wheels of the state forestry truck.

The inebriated man's truck was propelled back down the dirt road by the force of the collision. The old man's head punched through the windshield, which cut his chin and jaw in several places as it came back through. The bleeding made it look like his throat had been cut.

Upon getting out of the truck, the two hunters lay down on the shoulder of the road. They saw that the tandem wheels had been knocked out from under the forestry truck.

The forestry truck driver had a two-way radio in his truck, which he used to report the accident to the highway patrol. In short order, a patrol car rounded the curve and came sliding down the shoulder of the road toward the two hunters.

The Elder Statesman griped, "I had to get up and run with my throat cut."

The Excited Traveler

The blissful inattentiveness of people best described as social creatures engenders one situation after another where their minds capture just enough of the conversation going on around them to cause errors of ridiculous hilarity. The Elder Statesman, his wife (Lil), and their two daughters left Rough Edge going to Vicksburg to see the battlefield and the model of the Mississippi River at the Waterways Experiment Station. Their youngest daughter, Gina, was a social creature of the first rank. She was at the time about five years old and was very excited about the trip.

Coming onto Highway 84 from the Benton Springs Road, they turned left and soon came upon a sign pointing to Womack Hill. Lil asked about Womack Hill, and the Elder Statesman replied that the road came out in Gilbertville.

"When we get there, I will show it to you," he said.

After turning left onto Highway 7, they arrived at Gilbertville within ten minutes.

As they passed through the town, the Elder Statesman pointed to a sign and said, "That is where the road to Womack Hill comes out."

Gina, busy enjoying the sights of the town, perked up and said, "I want to see the road that the woman killed."

When he taught school, the Elder Statesman used to arrive at their apartment after work about an hour before Lil. He had usually watched a TV program called *Popcorn Cinema* while waiting for her to get home. On the trip to Vicksburg, they passed through a town that had a theater on the street they were traveling. The Elder Statesman saw the theater and commented, "There's the Popcorn Cinema." Gina came alive, shouting, "I want some cinnamon popcorn too."

Late in the afternoon, they arrived in Vicksburg. After inquiring at a service station while refueling the car, they were directed to the hotel where they had reservations. Three of the travelers were worn out after the all-day trip. Gina had taken a two-hour nap and was totally refreshed. After registering at the desk and getting the room key, they took the elevator up to their room. The Elder Statesman sat the suitcase down and unlocked the door.

Gina, the totally refreshed five-year-old first-time hotel guest, ran into the room, threw both arms out wide, and shouted, "Check it out now!"

The rest of the trip settled down into a learning experience for the children with visits to the Waterways Experiment Station, the civil war battlefield, the Balfour House, the Old Courthouse Museum, and the raised Civil War gunboat, the *USS Cairo*.

The Fifteen-Dollar Laugh

The western part of Rough Edge was growing rapidly. Coot's house-building project was part of that growth. It was located on Rub Board Lane, which was called that because of the bumpy road surface created by the frequent patching of potholes. The project had reached the stage of shingling the roof to make the building impervious to the effects of the weather. Coot set up a day when he was off work to get the job done.

Joe, a local young man that did odd jobs, was hired to help with the shingles. First they popped chalk lines so they could keep the runs of shingles straight. Then they put the bundles of shingles up onto the roof, spreading them out to be within easy reach when needed.

Coot explained to Joe, "All I want you to do is lay the shingles so that they are straight on the chalk lines. I am going to be right behind you nailing them in place. I don't want any crooked runs of shingles on my roof."

To be sure that Joe understood, Coot laid a few shingles along the chalk line and nailed them into place, explaining as he did so points to observe to keep them straight. Now they were ready to do some serious shingling.

Things progressed well for the first hour. Fatigue began to creep up on the two laborers, announced by the sweat stains cropping out on their shirts. Joe's concentration ebbed as the stains spread. Soon Coot began pointing out shingles that Joe had laid out of line.

Finally, Coot gruffly said, "Joe, if you lay one more shingle crooked, I am going to fire you!"

It wasn't long before Joe laid another shingle askew.

"Get off this roof, Joe! You're fired!" Coot said, pointing out the wayward shingle.

"Oh no! You don't mean that," Joe pleaded.

"Well," said Coot, "I'll let you go back to work for fifty cents, which I'll take out of your pay."

Time and again that day, Coot fired Joe but let him go back to work each time for fifty cents. The last of the shingles were nailed on a little before sundown.

"Get in the truck and I'll take you home," Coot directed Joe, telling him that he would pay him on Saturday.

Saturday arrived, and Coot went to settle up with Joe.

"Joe, I agreed to pay you fifteen dollars to help me shingle my house. I laid you off forty-two times, charging you fifty cents each time to go back to work. That comes to twenty-one dollars. Looks like you owe me six dollars."

Joe's mouth dropped open as he blurted, "Run that by me one more time."

Coot went through the explanation again.

Joe stammered, "Can you wait until next Saturday?"

Coot could restrain his laughter no longer. Taking out his wallet, he paid Joe his fifteen dollars, considering the laugh itself was worth that much.

The Gift

The Elder Statesman came home from work and, without saying a word to Lil, got out his tools, measured off the foundation, and began digging.

When Lil came outside and saw him digging in the yard, she demanded, "What is going on?

The Elder Statesman said, "Today is our thirtieth anniversary. Do you remember that patio you always wanted? Your thirty-year wait is over. I am going to build it for you. Just understand that I had to wait until those cedar trees we planted grew big enough to provide the patio with shade from the evening sun."

This was the first of two additions he would make to the house. The second was a bathroom with a walk-in closet off their bedroom, as well as a large utility room. Remodeling was not the Elder Statesman's favorite thing to do, but while adding the patio, he decided to close in the carport and make a dining room.

When all this work was complete, the old man took a day off to go fishing and relax. He and his cousin Sandy planned to go to Lake Marcel early Saturday morning and fish until noon. Early that morning, they loaded his boat onto the pickup, along with all their fishing gear. They were all set to go when he noticed the car.

Lil and the old man had a postal contract for the mail route out of the Rough Edge Post Office. All the stopping and starting on a mail route wore out a set of brake pads about every three months. Since he'd planned to go fishing on Saturday morning, the Elder Statesman had driven the car into the tractor shed and changed the brake pads on Friday afternoon. Just as he had completed the job, a student he tutored in algebra had driven up.

"Go on in. I'll be there as soon as I gather up my tools," the old man had said. Leaving the car at the tractor shed, he had gone to the house, washed up, and begun the tutoring session. By the time the session had ended, it was dark.

The next morning after loading the boat and fishing gear, the Elder Statesman saw the car at the tractor shed and told Sandy, "I am going to bring the car up to the house so it will be ready for Lil to run the mail route." He got into the car and made a U-turn to park in front of what once was a carport.

Anticipating a good day on the lake, the old man forgot about changing the brake pads the evening before. After changing the pads, the brakes must be pumped up before they will hold. When the Elder Statesman tried to stop the car, he realized he had not pumped up the brakes. He pumped furiously on the pedal, but to no avail. The car crashed into the dining room wall, caving it in and destroying a large picture window. The car did not get a scratch or dent on it. Lil came running out of the house, wondering what had happened.

After things were explained, Sandy and the old man went ahead with the fishing trip.

Sandy said to him, "When you went past me, I thought, *He's going to run into the house.* Then wham!"

A shocked Elder Statesman exclaimed, "Yes, and I don't like to remodel, but now I'll have to. Do you know what makes this incident so bad? After I hit the wall, the next time I pumped the petal, the brakes caught!"

The Lamentations of Hoot

H oot was the appellation that rode the back of a young man who lived across the highway from the Elder Statesman. His job as an electrician and instrument man made him one of the most valuable assets in Rough Edge. A series of misadventures in his younger days had prompted him to refer to any detrimental event as Hoot's luck.

The Elder Statesman agreed to help Hoot cut, split, and haul to his house a couple of loads of firewood. Early Saturday morning, they set forth on the wood-cutting expedition.

"We will go to Goat Hill and cut mostly blackjack oaks. There's a lot of them up at the top of the hill. My truck has a weak battery, so I am going to park it where we can roll it downhill to start it if necessary," Hoot said cheerfully.

After unloading saws, gas, oil, and a few tools, they set to work felling and cutting up blackjacks. By dinnertime, more than two loads lay on the ground.

"Let's get the truck, back it up to a pile of wood, and load it. Then we will take it home and eat dinner while we are there," Hoot said.

He got into the truck to back it up, but the battery was too weak to start it. He got out of the truck and said, "We will have to push it to get it rolling downhill to crank it."

Unnoticed by either of them, he had parked the truck with one of the front tires in a small washed-out depression. No matter how much they pushed, the truck would not budge from the depression.

"I'll get another battery, come back, put it in the truck, and haul the wood. Beats all, doesn't it? Here I am walking because I have a truck that will not roll downhill," bemoaned the unfortunate woodcutter.

A little later, another misadventure came calling on Hoot.

He was pulling old heart pine logs out of Benson's Creek, which he was having cut into sills for his house. Hoot was using his father-in-law's winch truck to pull the logs out. Some of them were stuck in the mud. To get those, he attached the winch cable to the end of the log and chained the other end of the truck to a tree. He tightened the winch up so that it held a continuous pull on the log. Hoot left the winch truck exerting tension on the log for several days. Usually when he returned, the log would be loose enough for him to pull it out of the creek. Then disaster struck!

After leaving the setup to go to work, he expected to retrieve a fine log when he returned. But one of those heavy thunderstorms hit around Churchwell, raising Benson's Creek several feet and putting the winch truck two-thirds under the water. The Elder Statesman picked up Hoot walking home after finding the winch truck partially submerged.

"I have three vehicles, yet here I am walking again. The winch truck is underwater, my pickup is at my father-in-law's house in Franklin, and my wife dropped me off out here before going to Jackson in our car. That's just Hoot's luck!" he exclaimed.

The Elder Statesman mused about Hoot's luck while laughing at the latest episode. He concluded that if all the bad luck stories his passenger told were written down in a single volume, it would be titled *The Lamentations of Hoot*. The Elder Statesman went to Jackson and purchased a picture frame, some two-inch gold letters, and a piece of black velvet cloth. He created a black background with the cloth and glued the gold letters to it, spelling "Hoot's Luck," with the *K* positioned in the corner on its side as if it had fallen. He inserted his creation into the frame and mailed it to Hoot.

When it arrived, Hoot opened it and howled with laughter. "I know the Elder Statesman sent me this," he chirped gleefully.

The Land of Distraught Temperaments

Most of the citizens of Rough Edge, especially the Elder Statesman—her husband—were well acquainted with the easily excited and highly explosive nature of the Gray-Headed Granny's temperament. The Elder Statesman often described the expression of a divergent point of view to hers as being like "punching a rattlesnake with a short stick." Her best friend noted that telling her a different opinion was often like "lighting a stick of dynamite with a short fuse." Her eruptive nature added a colorful spiciness to her activities and much zest to her engagements with the locals.

In the days when her children were young, she buzzed around the kitchen, preparing dinner so that it would be ready for the Elder Statesman when he got home from work. She was a great cook, taking pride in preparing dishes that he loved. Cornbread happened to be one item he relished above most other foods. Occasionally the cornbread would stick to the skillet, and when it did, her excitable nature broke out in force. First would come a violent shaking of the skillet in an attempt to dislodge the stubbornly clinging pone. Next, descriptive verbiage of the injuries she was going to inflict upon that complicit skillet assaulted the delicate ears of the children. Last of all, she jerked open a drawer, grabbed a knife, and attacked the offending loaf with a violence of which Jack the Ripper would have been proud. Of things not working as they should, the Gray-Headed Granny was most intolerant.

Sewing not being her strong suite, she was frustrated by the slightest difficulty she encountered in the pursuit thereof. The prolongation of her days brought forth a decline of her physical capabilities, of which diminished vision was most notable. One jolly Friday afternoon, after completing all the sewing on a dress that she could do on her machine, she sat down on the couch with the dress, a spool of thread, and a needle, intending to finish the job that day. Four or five attempts to thread the needle resulted in failure. The temperature of her excitable nature began to rise, manifesting itself in the tightening of her jaw as a grimace spread over her face.

The Gray-Headed Granny dropped the needle and thread in her lap. Looking around, she seized the first thing within reach—a pair of scissors—and viciously threw them across the room. The scissors impaled the dining room door.

The Elder Statesman asked, "Did that little fit of yours help anything?"

The temperature of her rage fell immediately to normal levels, and she quipped, "It made me feel better!"

Relieved, she and the old man broke out into a long, hardy laugh.

Consequences sometimes accompanied her visitations to the land of distraught temperament. The construction of their home some six years after their marriage ushered in a pile of waste trimmings from the building materials.

Glenda, the Elder Statesman's niece, was a teenage girl at the time. Being a prankster, she said, "Aunt Lil, are you afraid of frogs?"

"Yes I am," said Lil.

Having seen one on the wall of the house, Glenda grabbed it and put it down Lil's collar. The Gray-Headed Granny's temper flashed, reminiscent of the eruption of Mount St. Helens. She grabbed Glenda by the arm and, giving it a twist, threw her to the ground. With a strip of paneling from the waste pile, she explained to Glenda's posterior just how deeply she feared a frog! Regardless of the explanation, Glenda never stopped laughing.

The Loafers Table

The custom has become so widespread that it is now accepted as a great American institution. In many restaurants around the country, one large table is set aside for the waitresses to use when they are not busy. Most frequently, a number of retired people who are regular patrons of the restaurant gravitate to that table to chat and enjoy a cup of coffee. Such was the case at one of the local establishments in Rough Edge that the Elder Statesman frequented. Being the casual observer that he was, he designated that unique arrangement as the "Loafers Table."

Sean began going to that same eatery. Tragedy befell Sean. People at church began to notice a gradual drifting apart between Sean and his wife. Before long came the separation and then the divorce. Shortly thereafter, he began having breathing problems that resulted in him being declared disabled. Of course, that issued him into the ranks of the unemployed.

Without his wife's cooking and with plenty of time on his hands, Sean began eating out much of the time. Like so many other retired or disabled persons, he began inching his way toward the Loafers Table.

At first, he sat at a table far back in the corner. With time and after seeing other people he knew in the restaurant, he moved out to a table in the middle of the place. Then, as he became acquainted on a first name basis with the waitresses, he moved adjacent to the Loafers Table.

The Elder Statesman went to the restaurant for dinner one day, and lo, he espied Sean sitting at the previously mentioned table, gaily bantering with the waitresses and other loafers. After observing this behavior for several weeks, the Elder Statesman began jesting with Sean about his rapid acclimation into the loafers' ranks.

Every time he saw Sean, he said to him, "Be careful, Sean, or they will elect you chairman of the Loafers Table."

After several reminders to be careful, Sean asked the old man, "Just what do you have to do to be elected chairman?"

"That's really simple," said the Elder Statesman. "All you have to do is loaf more and better than any of the other patrons sitting at the Loafer's Table and the job is yours."

The Master Painter

The Elder Statesman and Lil became best friends
with Jane fifty years ago, and that friendship is still
just as strong today. Jane loved painting wildlife.
The old man saw some of her early work and realized that
she was a very talented artist. He encouraged her to contact
Ducks Unlimited about entering a duck stamp competition.
He very quickly discerned in her cranial cavity a commodious
section of ullage where confidence should have been. The
business of everyday life demanded so much of her time that
she had little opportunity to perfect her artistry.

A few years earlier, Jane had gone through a divorce and
moved from Rough Edge to Georgia to be near her family.
Years passed, accompanied by many changes, of which Jane
moving back to Jefferson was one, much to Lil's delight.

Louise, a friend in Mississippi, told the Elder Statesman
about a lady in Charlestown who was going to have a heart,
lung, and kidney transplant as soon as a donor could be
found. She was a farmer's wife, and they had no insurance,
so people in the Charlestown area were doing fundraising
events to help them. One of the fundraisers happened to
be an art auction. The old man approached Jane about

painting a picture and donating it to the cause. After much persuasion, she finally agreed to do it.

Lil and the Elder Statesman carried the painting to Mable, the lady in charge of the auction, on Labor Day. The painting was a nighttime scene of a cabin by a lake with a skein of Canadian geese overhead. Mable loved the painting saying, "This painting will do great because we have a lot of duck hunters in the area."

As the time for the auction approached, the Elder Statesman asked Jane if she would like to attend it.

"I would love to go, she replied.

The old man, his daughter Alexis, and Jane made the six-hour trip to Charlestown. They arrived at the Three Crowns Restaurant, where the auction was being held, an hour early so they could look over the works being sold. Jane's painting was displayed on one side of the sign describing the event.

The old man said to Jane, "By putting your painting by the sign, they must think it is very good."

The first painting did not sell because the bidding did not reach the artist's reserve, which was the minimum price for which the artist would sell it. Everything over that price went to the cause. The next four paintings sold, but the auctioneer was disappointed with the prices. Next they brought out Jane's painting.

The auctioneer commented, "We don't know much about the artist. She is self-taught and lives in Jefferson, Alabama. Who will bid a hundred dollars?"

The atmosphere in the restaurant became electric as the bidding shot up to $1,200. It came down to two men bidding. The painting sold for $1,700, which turned out to be the highest price a painting sold for at the auction.

The auctioneer said, "I am told that the artist is here tonight."

The Elder Statesman whispered, "Stand up, Jane. They want to know who you are."

When she stood, the crowd cheered her with a round of applause.

After the auction, Alexis, wandering around the room, came upon the man who bought the painting. "Would you like to meet the artist?" she asked. "She is with us. Come on and I will introduce her to you."

He told Jane, "I saw that painting on the internet, and I came here to buy it. It is very good!" When he left, a man he had been talking to stepped up and said, "My name is Roscoe Roberson. I am a vice president with Ducks Unlimited. We are always looking for new talent. Can you have me some more paintings to look at by February? I am going to Miami to a meeting and I would like to show them."

The Elder Statesman and Lil enjoyed many trips with Jane to art shows and to sign prints for Ducks Unlimited. The old man mused to himself, "I wonder if the master painter who turns the leaves red and gold in the autumn and drapes the evergreens with snow in winter reached down into the affairs of men to bless one good deed with another."

The OLRM

I n his younger days, the Elder Statesman worked as an inspector for a large corporation. That department was composed of twelve men, all college graduates and all as diverse as they possibly could be.

Tex was a very brash, irritating, short, heavyset, loudmouth who looked much like a cartoon character. Whenever he found anything that would not pass specs, he rejected it with an "I got you" attitude toward the production people. He delighted in making production people mad. No one liked for Tex to come into their units to work because although he was a good inspector, he had a bad attitude.

To reduce friction and keep the inspectors familiar with all areas of the plant and all the products made, they were rotated from area to area every three months. With the time to rotate approaching, Mack (the inspector in unit five) decided to have a little fun at the expense of the unit supervisor. Mack took a sheet of paper and with a felt-tip maker wrote on it, "The O.L.R.M. is coming." He then taped it up in a conspicuous place in unit five where he knew the unit supervisor would see it. Sure enough, the supervisor saw it and began to wonder what the OLRM was and why it was coming to his unit. He quizzed his foremen about it, but no one knew anything.

On Monday, a week before the rotation, Mack took another sheet of paper and wrote on it, "The OLRM will be here next week." He removed the previous sheet and taped the new one up in its place. When the supervisor saw it, he became very edgy. He made several calls to other supervisors around the plant to find out if they had any information concerning the OLRM. All his efforts proved unsuccessful.

Tex had a trail bike that he often rode after work. Three days before the inspectors were to rotate, Tex had a wreck on his bike and came to work the next day all bruised and scratched. Mack took another sheet of paper and wrote on it, "The OLRM is unsafe," and taped it up in the same place. One thing the company stressed was safety. When the supervisor saw that sign, he was panic-stricken. He was not going to allow anything into his unit that was unsafe.

Forgetting everything, he rushed into the office of the superintendent in charge of production, red-faced, huffing, and puffing. "What is this unsafe OLRM that is coming to my unit on Monday?" he demanded. "I'm not letting anything deemed unsafe into my unit. I don't care what it is or who is sending it!" he ranted.

"Take it easy. We will find out what is going on," replied the somewhat-shocked superintendent. He had seldom seen anyone as upset as the supervisor.

When the supervisor returned to the unit, one of the hourly men noticed how upset he was, so he asked, "What's wrong?"

"That unsafe OLRM will be here in the unit Monday, and I can't find anyone who knows anything about it," he growled.

"I think the Elder Statesman knows something about it. Why don't you ask him?" the hourly man said.

Immediately the supervisor sent for the Elder Statesman, and when he came into the office, he demanded of him, "What is the OLRM and why is it unsafe?"

The Elder Statesman laughed and said, "OLRM stands for Obnoxious Little Round Man. That's what all the other inspectors call Tex, and we say he is unsafe because he got all banged up when he wrecked his trail bike. If you are referring to that sign in the unit, Mack put that up."

First the supervisor turned red and then purple. He was nearly foaming at the mouth when he yelled, "You tell that **** Mack that I said for him never to put up another sign in my unit!" He didn't literally explode, and that was the miracle of it all.

The Proverbs
of a Father

A seventy-year-old Elder Statesman reminisced about an event during his teenage years that taught him the validity of one very important scripture. His grandfather was a lawyer from Birmingham. He had purchased a tract of land near Carter's Corner and moved there to live. For a while, they bottled the mineral water and sold it.

One day, the Elder Statesman and his father were riding around in a pickup, looking over the place, when they came up to a gate.

His father said to him, "Get out and open the gate."

The Elder Statesman got out, mumbling under his breath, "If you want the gate open, get out and open it yourself." Not realizing that his father had heard what he said, the teenager poked around as he approached the gate. Before he got there, his father got out of the truck, cut a gallberry switch, and caught him by the wrist. Therewith he administered proper instruction concerning the real meaning of Proverbs 13:24, which says, "He who spares the rod hates his son, but he who loves him disciplines him promptly" (NKJV).

The Elder Statesman mused, "I am seventy years old now, and I still run when I get out to open a gate."

Perhaps twenty years later, the Elder Statesman wanted to plant a green patch for the deer. There was a five-acre field that had been left idle for a few years and was overgrown with broom sage. The would-be planter plowed a two-disc-wide fire break all the way around the field.

His father, observing all that activity, inquired, "What are you doing, son?"

"I am plowing a fire break around this field so that I can burn it off and plant green stuff for the deer," he replied.

"I don't think I would burn it. That fire may get out and burn the woods," said his father.

"Oh no. I've got it with this fire break," answered the planter.

His father left him with the project and walked back home.

Getting off the tractor and walking all the way around the field, the Elder Statesman surveyed the plowed ground to be sure there was no place the fire could get out. Satisfied that all was well, he struck a match and lit the broom sage in several places. A right jolly blaze was proceeding across the field when the wind commenced to blow. The speed of the flames across the field increased to the point that a man could not outrun them. The flames reached the fire break and jumped it as if it wasn't there.

Reaching the tractor, the Elder Statesman saw that the fire had cut him off from the road. There was nothing to do but flee from the blaze down through the woods on the tractor. Alas, he came upon one of the numerous stream bottoms that traversed the place. He had to abandon the tractor. This particular branch bottom was covered with the green briars noted for long sharp thorns. The Elder Statesman got down on his belly and began to crawl through and under the briars. By the time he reached the point where the ground was damp, his shirt was ripped to shreds, the flesh underneath it was lacerated and bloody, and the flames were rapidly approaching. Soon the flames engulfed the tractor, burning every part of it that wasn't metal. That vicious orange monster came on down to the stream bottom and, burning the pine straw lodged in the briars above the bleeding Elder Statesman, marched right over him and the bottom. It was finally halted by Cedar Creek.

Many years later when recounting the experience, the Elder Statesman wistfully said, "Proverbs 1:1 in the New King James Version says, 'A wise son listens to the instruction of his father.'" He moaned. "I learned the hard way. That is one of the most valid statements ever made."

The Snows of Yesteryear

The Elder Statesman lived on a hilltop in Rough Edge across Highway 24 from Ole E.D. Their family dwellings had been thus juxtaposed since the 1930s. Through the Great Depression and World War II, their families developed into good, solid, dependable friends. Time marched on and Ole E.D. grew up, finished high school, and went to MSU. Many adventures peppered his days there, one most somber.

In his junior year, Claude, a friend from Mobile, became his roommate. Claude was attending school on an athletic scholarship as a pitcher on the baseball team. For most of the baseball season that year, conflicts in class schedules had prevented Ole E.D. from seeing Claude play. It worked out that on the evening of March 21, 1963, things lined up and Ole E.D. went to the baseball park to watch Claude. Sitting in the stands, he saw the car of the chief of the campus police pull up and park.

When the chief got out and headed for the stands, an anxious, apprehensive feeling came over Ole E.D. His eyes followed Chief Hood as he entered the park gate and began asking students questions. Finally, he arrived at Ole E.D.'s seat on the end of the bleacher and asked him, "Are you E.D. _____?"

When he affirmed that he was, Chief Hood said without any explanation, "You will have to come with me!" Once in the car, the chief said, "You have to make a call home."

Ole E.D. looked at Chief Hood and said, "My father is dead, isn't he?"

"I don't know," were the last words said in the car as the two rode to the chief's office, where E.D. called home.

His mother told him that his father had been accidentally electrocuted and he would have to come home for the funeral.

"I could have told you," said Chief Hood as he placed a hand on the shoulder of the weeping young man, "but your mother wanted to tell you herself."

The Elder Statesman was sitting in his truck in front of the house when Ole E.D. arrived home. He got out of his truck, walked over to the sad young man, and said to him, "I can't go inside because I'm old and have heart trouble and because your dad was one of the best friends I ever had."

The emotional strain of speaking to his friend's son clearly showed on the old man's face as tears trickled down his cheeks. Those days composed the saddest time of Ole E.D.'s life, but they too, like the snows of yesteryear, passed.

A few weeks later, Ole E.D. returned home for the weekend. The Elder Statesman found out that he was home and that he was returning to school on Sunday morning. He went down his driveway, got his Sunday paper out of his mailbox, and sat reading it in his truck while he waited for

Ole E.D. to come out of the driveway across the highway from him. Upon seeing the young man coming down the driveway, the Elder Statesman stepped out of his truck and flagged him over.

With emotion cracking his voice, he said, "Your dad was a good man and a good friend. I will see to it that you have what you need to finish college. Just let me know when you need anything."

Fifty-six years later, the impact of those words still resides in Ole E.D.'s heart. The main goal of his life became being a friend like the Elder Statesman.

The Sweetest Lesson

S ixty-five years ago, when the Elder Statesman was a twelve-year-old boy, two things happened in June that he looked forward to with great anticipation. School was out for the summer and ripe red and yellow plums hung in profusion from bushes in numerous groves around Rough Edge.

Early one morning before the sun rose high in the sky and heated the air until it was insufferably hot, the Elder Statesman was leaning on the slab fence around Aunt Lucy's garden. Aunt Lucy was a large woman who moved with a slow shuffling gait. She wore a blue dress that came down to her ankles, a starched and ironed white apron, and a bandanna folded into a triangle on her head, the three corners of which were tied in a knot in the center of her forehead.

She spied the boy leaning on her fence, and in a high nasal twang asked, "What do you want?"

The surprised boy replied, "May I come into your garden and get a few plums off of your trees?"

"No, you may not." Aunt Lucy scowled. "You will tromp all over my vegetables and be climbing the trees, breaking limbs off of them. Besides, there are many other groves where you can get all the plums you want."

The two trees in Aunt Lucy's garden were the largest in Rough Edge, standing more than twenty feet tall. Those two trees produced the biggest and sweetest plums found anywhere in Rough Edge, which was the reason the boy wanted some of those particular plums. The Elder Statesman knew that the plums found at the very top of the tree were bathed with the most morning dew and kissed with the most golden sunlight. Thus, the sweetest plums always grew at the top of the tree. Aunt Lucy knew the boy would climb the tree to get those plums.

"Some way, I am going to fix Aunt Lucy for not letting me have any plums," mused the angered lad.

Before long, he decided upon the perfect way to aggravate Aunt Lucy. Her house was one of those two-room affairs. About forty-feet long and fourteen-feet wide, it was weathered to a gray patina, having never seen a drop of paint. The windows had no glass in them but were covered with wooden doors that she opened during the day. The roof was tin, the galvanization of which had been replaced long ago with brown rust. The mischievous boy took his BB gun out to the brush-covered hillside overlooking Aunt Lucy's garden and house and, hiding in the bushes, began to pelt the rusty roof of the hovel with BB pellets.

Before long, Aunt Lucy's sweat-covered face appeared in a window, from which she yelled, "You boys had better quit shooting my roof! You are going to make it leak!"

Success! Aunt Lucy was aggravated! The Elder Statesman went on his way, seeking other adventures.

About a week later, looking out his back door, the boy saw Aunt Lucy shuffling along with her huckleberry walking stick. It was obvious when she opened his family's garden gate that she was coming to their house. Hearing a knock at the door, his mother saw that Aunt Lucy's black face was streaked with sweat from the exertion of moving her heavy body along the quarter-mile trek.

"Come in, Lucy, and I'll fix us a cup of coffee," cooed Lola.

They chatted over the coffee for half an hour.

Aunt Lucy finally came to the point of her visit. "Those boys muddied up my spring. It is hard for me to go to the spring for water, and if it is muddied up, I have to go home and wait for it to clear up and then make another trip. Will you get those boys to leave the spring alone?"

The boy expected his mother to throw Aunt Lucy out, but she did not. All she did was say, "I'll take care of it."

The Elder Statesman had not bothered the spring, and being falsely accused angered him to the nth degree. Actually, the only reason he had not muddied the spring was because he had not thought of it.

Lola knew a fact that her son did not know. Aunt Lucy was a diabetic and had a hard time getting food that she could eat. From that day on for the rest of the summer, twice a week Lola fixed a plate from her table and a glass of tea for Aunt Lucy. The Elder Statesman was given the privilege of carrying that plate and tea to her. His temper was steaming every step of the way, hotter than the sand in the road.

"She falsely accuses me and I carry her dinner," he ranted to himself.

Summer finally ended, and the Elder Statesman went back to the school. Between school, homework, and chores, he had little time for mischief.

The school year passed quickly and vacation began. In June, the Elder Statesman saw Aunt Lucy ambling along through their garden. *Not another summer of conflict with Aunt Lucy*, he thought. Lola invited her in for coffee again, and after Lucy sat a cloth-covered syrup bucket on the table, they sat chatting for a while.

Lucy said as she removed the cloth from the bucket, "I thought the boys might like a few plums from my trees." The bucket was full of big golden, sweet plums ready for the pesky boys.

Later in years, the Elder Statesman realized that his mother had taught him that treating people with kindness was a much sweeter thing that the plums that grow in the top of the tree.

The Treaty of Rough Edge

The matrimonial bliss in the Elder Statesman's household suffered occasional disruptions. One such interruption concerning the distribution of the family's financial resources exposed the forcefulness of the involved parties' personalities.

Later at work, the Elder Statesman was complaining to Fred about the situation. He was taken aback when Fred revealed, "My wife and I never argue about money."

"How did you achieve that happy state of affairs?" inquired the old man.

"What is your job here?" asked Fred.

"I receive, warehouse, and ship these chemical products," answered the old man.

"The company gives you everything you need to do your job," Fred stated. Then he asked, "What is your wife's job?"

"She runs the house," said the Elder Statesman, sensing where the conversation was going.

"Give her the money she needs to do her job, with the provision that if she runs out of money, she borrows from you, and if you run out, you borrow from her. Also, all the household bills must be paid first, and if she has any money left over, she can spend it however she chooses with no questions asked," Fred told him.

The Elder Statesman went home and related Fred's advice to the Gray-Headed Granny. He requested, "Figure up how much money you need to run the house and bring me the numbers. I am going to give you that amount each month. You can spend it anyway you like with no questions asked so long as the bills are paid and no checks bounce."

The Gray-Headed Granny loved the arrangement. Thus began the hammering out of the provisions of the Treaty of Rough Edge, the first being the adoption of the new financial arrangement, which has remained in force ever since. From time to time, disruptions to the domestic tranquility between the old man and the Gray-Headed Granny have necessitated the addition of other provisions to the Treaty of Rough Edge.

The Gray-Headed Granny loves flowers. She planted them randomly all over the yard. When the Elder Statesman mowed the grass, he wore himself out dodging around all those flowers. When he complained to her about the difficulties the flowers caused, she displayed an air of hurt feelings. The old man poured cement sidewalks around three sides of the house and left space between the walks and the house for flower beds. He also formed stone beds around the trees in the yard and constructed three stone crescent-shaped beds, giving her a total of seventeen flower beds.

Upon completion of the beds, the second provision of the Treaty of Rough Edge was adopted. The Gray-Headed Granny would remove all the random flowers from the yard and transplant them into the beds. She could plant any and all the flowers she wanted within the beds, with the Elder Statesman assisting her. No flowers were to be planted anywhere on the place except in the beds. Peace descended and reigned supreme once again in Rough Edge.

The Elder Statesman is cold in nature, while the Gray-Headed Granny generates enough heat to melt the polar ice caps. The thermostat had been adjusted so many times that the paint had worn off most of it. Expressing the condition of being hot or cold had sparked many vituperative outbursts between the two. The acquisition of an electric blanket with dual controls eased part of the tension, but not all. The adoption of the third provision of the Treaty of Rough Edge created an uneasy cessation of the thermostat dispute. That provision gave control of the thermostat to the Gray-Headed Granny from May 1 until November 1 and to the Elder Statesman from November 1 until May 1. Neither party is allowed to complain about the temperature while the thermostat is in the other party's control. Neither are they allowed to change the setting. Jerusalem shall be a cup of trembling (Zech. 12:2 KJV), and so is the temperature in the Elder Statesman's house.

The Trouble
with the Dome

The gentleman, Malinoski, was of Polish extraction. When he got his hair cut, the clippers circumnavigated three-fourths of his head. The higher elevations were completely barren. He was a big man who loved to mingle with the crowds in many of the watering holes in Mobile. The alcohol he consumed induced much sweating when Malinoski put forth physical exertion at work after a night on the town. Indeed, the late-night hours in the bars brought forth other habits as well.

Each day, after a quick bite to eat, Malinoski settled down in one of the chairs in the Elder Statesman's office for a much-needed nap. October was a beautiful, clear fall of the year month, yet it was still very warm. The Elder Statesman passed out to each man in his crew a bright yellow hard hat liner in preparation for the cooler weather that was coming in a few weeks. Malinoski snapped the liner into his hard hat shortly before going to load drums in a trailer.

As usual, he sweated copiously. He returned to the office and ate his quick bite of lunch. Taking off his hard hat, he settled down for a nap. The Elder Statesman could not help but laugh at the sight he beheld. The sweat had caused the liner to fade, dyeing the higher elevation above Malinoski's ears the same bright yellow hue as the hard hat liner. To end that problem, he washed the liner in hot water until no more excess dye tinged the water. He then went to the change room showers and scrubbed his cranial dome until the thin covering of skin was burnished a bright red.

The next week, one of the men in the crew had to stencil some drums for shipment. Before leaving the office, he poured some black stencil ink on the stencil roller. He then proceeded to run the roller up and down the side of one of the file cabinets to cover the roller uniformly with ink. Just before lunch break, out he went to stencil the drums. Within ten minutes, Malinoski came into the office, ate his bite of lunch, and settled down for a nap. After he went to sleep, his head flopped over against the freshly inked file cabinet. Malinoski woke up twenty minutes later, stretched, and looked around the office. The Elder Statesman nearly fell out of his chair when he looked at him. The whole side of his head was coated with the black stencil ink.

The Elder Statesman exclaimed, "Malinoski, you just can't make up your mind whether you want to be black, yellow, or white!"

Through the Eyes of Alcohol

Don't gaze at the wine, seeing how red it is, how it sparkles in the cup, how smoothly it goes down. For in the end, it bites like a poisonous snake. You will see hallucinations and you will say crazy things.
—Proverbs 23:31—33, NKJV

The Elder Statesman, being a casual observer of the human species for many years, described the wife of Penrod as a rotund individual. Penrod himself was a politician of some renown in the county where his domicile was located. Having the mindset of a public servant, Penrod joined and became a very active member of the Civil Air Patrol.

The report of a missing aircraft in the northwest quadrant of the county was submitted to the Civil Air Patrol, and a search was initiated. Penrod and the Elder Statesman took off in a small plane to search the area around Penrod's house. Penrod had consumed a good part of a fifth of whiskey prior to takeoff and had concealed the remainder in the bottle under his jacket. By the time they reached the search area, he was intoxicated. The Elder Statesman piloted the plane over Penrod's house.

"Look there!" exclaimed the inebriated politician. "I see the parachute of the pilot of that missing plane dangling there, blowing in the breeze."

Before the old man could stop him, Penrod radioed news of the discovery back to the base. A ground team was sent out to investigate. One of the team members was a reporter for the local newspaper. The headline he drafted for the next edition of the paper read: "Local politician misidentifies his wife's undergarments hanging on a clothesline as the parachute of missing plane's pilot."

Penrod was an avid deer hunter who often joined other enthusiasts hunting along the upper reaches of Tauler Creek. He thrived on the heated debates awash in the political spectrum but could not tolerate the biting cold of a frosty morning. Once on his stand, he often built a fire to warm his exterior and began taking deep drafts from the bottle of whiskey he brought with him to warm his interior parts.

Before long, he was just a little unsteady. The other hunters saw smoke rising up from Penrod's stand. His fire had gotten out, and by the time the other hunters got there, over an acre of woods had burned. The intoxicated Penrod was standing on a stump in the middle of the burned area, giving a political speech. The fire had completely consumed the stock of his gun, which he had leaned against a nearby tree. A hunter in his condition didn't need to have a gun anyway.

The anguish of an empty refreshment bottle so disturbed Penrod that he procured a twenty-five-gallon keg of brew from his local supplier. Being the extroverted politician that he was, he invited Bob to go with him to the place where he stowed the keg for a drink. After imbibing, the two men secreted the keg once again in the brush. That night, Bob returned to the scene, stole the keg, and hid it in a new place.

The next day, Bob took Henry to the new hideout, where they both became so unsteady that they could hardly hide the keg. Henry, not willing to forego the pleasure of consuming the keg's contents, retrieved the keg and hid it yet again. Not knowing the history of the keg, Henry invited Penrod to go with him for a drink. Penrod was not one to turn down such an opportunity. Thus, the keg was duly tapped and the fiery liquid heavily sampled.

Penrod did not recognize his own keg. Under the cover of darkness, he returned to the scene and stole his own keg of whiskey!

Weak Eyes

A culture tends to develop around activities in which a limited number of connoisseurs participate. Their vocabulary, when engaged in their particular activity, constricts to a saltiness of oft-repeated words and phrases. In the world of pool players, for example, a "whale" refers to a person who has a lot of money to lose and who does not play very well. A "fish" is anyone you can beat and that you can talk into playing for money. The players themselves, in the course of their playing careers, earn a sobriquet by which they are known ever after.

There was a player in Rough Edge in a five-dollar game of nine ball with three others. Willard ran the balls from the four through the eight. The game-winning nine ball was about six inches from the pocket, and Willard left the cue ball about six inches from the nine and straight in. After aiming at the nine for more than a minute, Willard shot and missed the nine by a couple of inches.

The Elder Statesman, sitting on a bench under the windows, chided Willard, "Even Ray Charles would have made that shot, and he's blind!"

"Oh well," responded Willard. "That's not the worst shot I ever made."

From that time on, he was known as Worst Shot Willard.

The Elder Statesman's brother Bo had a natural talent for pool. By the time he was sixteen years old, very few local players could beat him. He became one of the top four or five players in the counties around Rough Edge. By virtue of the fact that Bo wore glasses, the other players called him Weak Eyes. Other players from outside of his area often came to Rough Edge looking for a money game.

One day in the middle of the week, Bo was in the local billiard parlor, sitting on a bench, reading the paper. He and the owner happened to be the only people there when in walked a gentleman of African descent who inquired if Bo wanted to play some nine ball for ten dollars a game. Bo laid the paper down, selected a house cue, and agreed to play. Although the stranger was a very good player, in an hour and a half, Bo had won all his money.

The stranger put his cue in its case and, leaning over, placed both hands on the table and said, "Don't tell me! Don't tell me! You are the one they call Weak Eyes!"

Bo answered, "That's what they call me."

"When I left Mobile to come up here, they told me to play anybody but Weak Eyes. You can't beat him, they said." The loser groaned.

The pool culture has some additional features. An unwritten code among money players demanded that you never left a player whose money you took completely broke. Weak Eyes pulled out his winnings and returned to the stranger enough money for gas to go back to Mobile and a hundred-dollar stake.

When Country
Went to City

I n the yesteryears of the village of Rough Edge, very primitive conditions were manifested everywhere. Roads were little more than rutted-out tracks through the forested wilderness. Running water and indoor plumbing were unheard of conveniences. No one even conceived of having electricity in their home. Occasional contact with the more advanced communities and cities made folks in Rough Edge aware of those things, but they were not familiar with how they worked.

The Elder Statesman and Henry were twin brothers who operated a turpentine business that necessitated the occasional trip to Mobile. When country went to city, they sampled some of the strong flavors of drinks and under their influence exhibited such rowdy behavior that the police deposited them in the city jail.

The Elder Statesman and Henry spoke with a pronounced Southern accent that was about a yard long. The police asked them where they were from.

"We are from Rough Edgeeeee," Henry replied, stretching out the word *edge* the full yard that his accent allowed.

"And what is the population of that place?" the officer wanted to know.

"Oh, it's mostly pines and oaks like it is down here," the Elder Statesman said.

They were escorted to a cell to sleep off the effects of their celebrations in one of Mobile's many watering holes. Sometime after midnight, the Elder Statesman woke up thirsty. He called the jailer and requested some water.

"Just turn on the faucet and you can get all you want," said the jailer.

Having never seen a faucet before, the old man persuaded the jailer to turn it on for him. He drank and drank and drank until he could drink no more. Then, not knowing how to turn the water off, the Elder Statesman called out, "Henry, come over here and drink some water before we both drown!"

Where's the Cat?

There were no greater cat lovers in Rough Edge than Ole E.D. and his wife, Lillian. For all the years of their life together, they had one or two cats as pets. Each cat had its own unique personality. They had a part Siamese named Willie, who was the most unique of all.

Ole E.D. had a small muscadine vineyard from which he sold fruit to grocery stores and to people who came and picked their own. The Elder Statesman came out to the vineyard and inquired about picking some muscadines before Ole E.D. opened it up to the public. The old gentleman wanted to make a batch of wine with which to warm his inward parts on cold winter nights.

"I'll call you when they are ready and before I open up for business," said Ole E.D.

Three weeks later, Ole E.D. called the Elder Statesman to inform him that the muscadines were ripe enough for him to pick. "I have not yet mowed between the rows of vines, nor have I trimmed the vines, but you are welcome to get what you need," he said to his friend.

The next day, one excited old man arrived at the vineyard. Ole E.D. showed him a row of vines that had a lot of ripe fruit. The Elder Statesman sat his bucket down by the first vine in the row, and after looking carefully for a rattler in the tall grass, he began to pick the fruit. As he proceeded down the row, he became so engrossed in picking that he forgot about looking for rattlers.

Willie had followed them out to the vineyard and crept unnoticed under the first vine. When the Elder Statesman reached the place where Willie was hiding, that cat jumped out from under the vine, wrapped himself around the Elder Statesman's leg, and sank his claws in to hold on. The old man just knew that a rattler had gotten him. Down that row he hopped on one leg, violently shaking the other in a vain attempt to dislodge Willie. All the while, he was screaming at the top of his lungs. Ole E.D. had never seen such an exhibition of acrobatic maneuvering in his life. The cat finally let go, and the old man paused for several minutes to catch his breath and recover his wits before he finished picking his bucket full of fruit.

Ole E.D. and the Elder Statesman often got together to cook fish, taking turns at each other's house. The old man, having caught several bass, rode out to Ole E.D.'s to arrange a time to cook them. Ole E.D. was not at home, but he had left his shop door open. Noticing the open door and the pool table inside, the old man decided to knock a few pool balls around while he waited for Ole E.D. to return. The shop had exposed ceiling joists and a bench across the end opposite the door. When the shop door was left open, Willie often went in, jumped up on the bench, and then jumped up on a ceiling joist, where he spent most of the day.

The old man wound up with a shot where he had to bend over with his back to the bench. Willie hopped down unseen from the joist to the bench and then hopped again, landing in the middle of the old man's back. The Elder Statesman was so frightened that he pitched his pool cue through the door and twenty feet into the yard. Ole E.D. soon came home, and plans were finalized for the cookout.

The Elder Statesman and his wife, Dixie, arrived on the appointed day. She took a seat on the sofa while Lillian, Ole E.D., and the old man stirred about, lighting the cooker, getting the fish ready, and putting oil in the pot that was on the cooker. The door out to the patio, where the cooker was located, had been left open. Naturally, Willie went into the house. Ole E.D. came in to get a bowl to put the fish in once they were cooked. He saw Dixie standing up, punching at Willie, who was on the back of the sofa, with her walking stick.

"What's going on?" asked Ole E.D.

"That cat hopped up on the back of the sofa and pulled my hair," she said.

Willie was promptly evicted and the door was closed.

Some weeks later, the Elder Statesman pulled up in front of Ole E.D.'s house in his pickup. Seeing Ole E.D. sitting on his patio, the old man opened his truck door, put one foot on the ground, and stood up. In that position, he looked all around the place.

"Where's the cat?" he demanded. "I keep my eye on that cat!"

White Coveralls

Mason, a gentleman of African descent, was a very vocal individual who was well-liked by all his coworkers and most of the citizens of Rough Edge. He had, by hard work and careful management, bought and paid for eighty acres of land near the Elder Statesman's farm. Mason was in the process of turning the cutover tract into a productive farm.

Although Mason worked at the same plant as the Elder Statesman, he was in a production unit that issued the workers white coveralls to work in. In time, Mason carried a set of well-worn coveralls home to wear when working about his place. The state mental hospital in Mt. Vernon was but a few miles through the woods from Mason's land. The patients at the hospital were also issued white outfits to wear. Confusion loomed upon the horizon.

One of the patients at the hospital escaped from the hospital's grounds. The staff searched for him for a few hours before reporting the escape to local law enforcement personnel. He was nowhere to be found at the hospital, so law enforcement officials were requested to keep a lookout for an African American male dressed in white anywhere near the mental hospital. An officer patrolling the highway between

Carter's Corner and Mt. Vernon passed by Mason's place. He spied Mason dressed in the white coveralls, working at clearing brush from some of his land. The officer believed he had found the escaped mental patient, so he wheeled into Mason's driveway to capture him.

Over very loud protesting and claims that this was his land, the officer handcuffed Mason, carried him to jail, and locked him up until the hospital could send someone to pick him up. Mason loudly demanded that they call any of several persons he named to come and identify him.

"Sure, you own that land. Sure, you are not a mental patient," the officers said, not believing Mason.

The louder he protested, the more the officers were convinced that he was mentally unbalanced.

A few hours after his capture, hospital personnel arrived at the city jail, whereupon they informed the officers that the man they had was not the missing patient. Mason decidedly did not enjoy his three-hour stint in jail.

When he came back to work, the Elder Statesman chided Mason, "See, I told you that you shouldn't have taken those overalls."

"From now on, I am going to sit on the front pew in church. If they ever take me to jail again, it will be for singing too loud," said Mason in response.

Wild Turkey and Pickle Juice

To say Henry was a large man would be the understatement of the year. Hardly a bathroom scale in Rough Edge could weigh him. It is not surprising that he got stuck when he tried to go under his house to repair a leaking water pipe. The Elder Statesman went over to Henry's house to see if he wanted to go to the Alabama football game on Saturday. He came upon the scene of Henry's son with a shovel, trying to dig a space deep enough under him so that he could wiggle out from under his house. That objective was finally achieved, and a dirty, scratched Henry clambered to his feet.

"Do you want to go to the Alabama game Saturday? We have four tickets and two bottles of whiskey. We need you to go and drive for us," said the Elder Statesman.

"Help me get this leaking pipe fixed and I will be glad to go and drive," replied Henry.

The Elder Statesman and two more of his friends planned to drink one bottle on the way to the game and the other on the way back. They needed a driver to get them to the game and back home safely.

The day of the game arrived, and the four departed their home station. As the number of miles they traveled increased, the level in the first bottle decreased. By the time they had traveled the 160 miles to Tuscaloosa, the contents of the first bottle had been gone for some time. Henry took the tickets, got them through the gate, and led his somewhat unsteady friends to their seats. How much of the game they saw and what the final score was, the Elder Statesman and his two other friends could not remember, but they all agreed that they had a roaring good time.

Over the course of the three-hour-long ball game, the effects of the first bottle subsided greatly. They anticipated returning to the car and the other bottle much more than they had anticipated seeing the ball game. It takes some time to extricate oneself from Tuscaloosa after an Alabama football game. The contents of the second bottle was more than half-gone by the time they got out of town. They had traveled less that fifty miles south on Highway 43 when the bottle ran dry. They settled back to sleep a little on the way home, but the Elder Statesman suffered an aggravating discomfiture that kept him awake: he had come down with a case of hiccups.

After a half hour passed with no sign of them letting up, he said to Henry, "The next place you see where I can get some water, stop. These hiccups are driving me crazy."

After twenty more miles, they came to a bar in a small town, and Henry stopped.

The Elder Statesman left the car, went into the bar, and sat down on a stool between two other patrons. "I've got the hiccups, and I need a glass of water to get rid of them," he said to the bartender.

"Oh, you don't want water. That will not get rid of the hiccups. What you need is some pickle juice," the bartender replied.

"Well, give me a glass of pickle juice," demanded the suffering man.

Within moments, the bartender sat down a glass of pickle juice in front of him. For a few minutes he sat there sipping his pickle juice, not knowing that the two men he had sat down between were in the middle of a fierce disagreement. The Elder Statesman looked around at the man on his left and was terrified to be looking down the barrel of a .45 pistol. The man on the left was trying to aim around his head to shoot the man on his right.

When dramatically relating this story to me, the Elder Statesman cried, "That was the quickest I ever lost the hiccups."

You Clean the Fish

The Elder Statesman suffered from the incurable malady of fishingitis. Since three-fourths of the earth is covered by water, he swore that God intended for a man to go fishing three out of every four days. There were times when he tried to live up to that intended purpose. He and his friend Bill arranged a fishing expedition for Monday morning. It started off a disaster and got worse as the day progressed.

"He made me mad the very first thing," growled Bill later. "He came to the house early to get a cup of coffee. He was whistling when he came in and that woke my wife up. She was less than a happy camper."

"I don't know what we are going to do," said Bill. "My outboard motor is on the blink. It will not start."

"Not to worry." The Elder Statesman chuckled. "We can take my power unit." That required a trip back to his house.

Bill pulled up in front of the Elder Statesman's shop.

"I'll only be a minute," the old man said as he disappeared into the shop.

He came out with a 1925 model five-horsepower motor. It had the gas tank on top and was started with a crank cord that you wound around a spool with a notch in it. Through years of overuse, the steering handle had broken off. In its place, the Elder Statesman had clamped on a two-foot piece of hoe handle.

"I'll be ready to go as soon as I mix up some oil and gas for the motor," the old man announced.

With the motor and gas loaded on the back of the truck, they were off for Bensons Creek. For several miles above the mouth of the creek, it was large enough to use an outboard motor if one was careful to avoid the logs and stumps. They unloaded the boat and launched it. The Elder Statesman put his power unit on the transom with the can of gas beside it. Then they loaded coolers, bait, lunches, and fishing gear.

At last we are ready to go, Bill thought to himself.

"Dad burn that Bobo. He has taken my crank cord," ranted the old man. "But that's no problem. I see the end of a trot line across the creek. Paddle me over there, and I'll make a crank cord out of it."

Bill paddled across the creek, and the jolly old gent cut a length of the cord, doubled it, and tied the ends together. He placed the knotted end inside the spool and, bringing the cord out through the notch, wound the cord around the spool. The second time he pulled the cord, the motor fired up. Alas, the knot in the cord hung in the notch of the spool. The whirling cord whipped the Elder Statesman's butt much more severely than his daddy ever had. Red welts lined the backs of his legs and behind. Once that situation was corrected, they went down the creek.

It turned out to be a good day for fishing. By midday, they had a great catch of bream on ice in the cooler. Tying up to a small cypress tree protruding out of the water, they broke out their lunches and consumed them while carrying on a lot of small talk. After lunch, they untied and started back upstream to the landing. All at once, the boat passed over one of those submerged logs. The foot of the motor hit the log. It then became evident that the Elder Statesman had forgotten to tighten the clamps to the transom. The motor jumped off the transom and sank into the inky black water.

"Oh no!" lamented Bill. "We will be after dark getting back to the landing."

The Elder Statesman got a deep breath, leaned over the transom, and with his knees holding him and his rear up in the air, plunged into the water. He soon came up and with one hand pulled himself back into the boat. With the other hand, he hauled in the motor.

With water streaking down his face, he grinned and said, "Don't worry. This is not the first time that this has happened. I'll have us going in a few minutes."

Grabbing a towel, he dried off the motor, took out the spark plug and dried it, drained the gas, and put fresh gas in the tank. Then he put the motor on the transom. This time, he tightened the clamps. After the forth pull of the makeshift crank cord, the motor sputtered to life.

When they got home, the Elder Statesman said to Bill, "I have half drowned trying to find that motor, and I have had my butt beaten by that crank cord. If you don't mind, I am going to leave these fish with you to clean."

The Elder Statesman never did like to clean fish, not even the ones he caught.

You Win!

For four years, Jerry Sparks dedicated himself to removing tranquility from the second floor of the C section of Hoyle Hall, a dormitory at MSU. He had turned all the showers wide open and plugged all the drains with towels. When the Elder Statesman returned to the dorm, water was cascading down the stairs. Opening his room, 212-C, he found that water had come in under the door and covered the floor. Where the pipes to the sink came through the floor, water was dripping on objects in the room below. The entire second floor was flooded.

From a nearby bowling establishment, Sparks had pilfered eight bowling pins. He and his roommate set up three pins at each end of the hall. They each had a pin, which they threw down the length of the hall, trying to knock down the three-pin setups. For several hours, neither study nor sleep took place on the second floor of the C section of Hoyle Hall. Sparks and his roommate were the only two who considered the bowling pin escapade great fun.

Doors to the dorm rooms opened to the inside. Sparks took a pair of pliers and twisted a coat hanger around the doorknobs of the two rooms directly across the hall from each other. He then took a broom handle, ran it through the free end of the coat hangers, and twisted them until they were taut. All this was done late Friday night after the room occupants were asleep, purposely attempting to keep those four students in their rooms over the weekend.

Time moved on.

Sparks and his roommate were in their room, studying for a final exam in a course they needed to graduate at the end of the semester. Upon discovering what Sparks was doing, several of the students with memories of all Sparks's disruptions of their studies met in the Elder Statesman's room.

The leader of the conspirators said, "Tonight is the night we are going to pay Sparks back for all his escapades over these last four years."

One of the plotters took a smoke bomb, rolled it under Sparks's door, and ducked into the room next door. Sparks and company charged out into an empty hall. The obscenities they shouted were not chronicled in a sailor's lexicon. The rest of the conspirators were in the Elder Statesman's room, laughing uproariously. They decided to give Sparks an hour to settle down before implementing phase two.

At midnight, the light in Sparks's room was still shining under the door. Another schemer took a long pack of firecrackers, lit the fuse, pushed them under the door, and ducked into a nearby room. In the midst of the crescendo of explosions, Sparks shot out of the room, threatening mayhem and bodily injury to the person who had dared to interrupt his studying. He and his roommate devised a foolproof plan to end what they had come to realize was payback time.

They placed two chairs back-to-back out in the hall under the light. They got their study materials and commenced once again to pour over books and notes, knowing that if any further shenanigans were attempted, they would see the culprit. Meanwhile, in the Elder Statesman's room, the gang was plotting their next move.

Claude, a pitcher on the baseball team, said, "One of you guys go to the bathroom and open the window. There is no screen on those windows. I will go outside and throw a cherry bomb through the window. It will rattle them good and proper."

The window was opened. The missile sailed through the window, bounced through the bathroom door, and exploded under Sparks's chair. The other participants were all standing in the hall to observe the operation.

When the reverberations died away, Sparks shouted to the group, "You win. I can't study!" He went into his room, turned out the light, and went to bed.

The next day, Sparks's professor listened to his explanation and agreed to let him take his final three days after the end of the semester.

The mill of God grinds slow, but it grinds exceedingly fine.